Assassins Of The Dead 3: Society Against Vampires

Assassins Of The Dead 3: Society Against Vampires

Avril Sabine

Cracked Acorn Productions
Australia

Assassins Of The Dead 3: Society Against Vampires

Published by

Cracked Acorn Productions

PO Box 1365

Gympie, Queensland 4570

Australia

978-1-925617-83-2 (Kindle)

978-1-925617-84-9 (EPUB)

978-1-925617-85-6 (Print)

Genre: Young Adult Fantasy/Paranormal

Cover design by Caitlyn Petersen

Some heroes work in the shadows, only their deeds remembered.

The Society Against Vampires are in Dreyton and vampires are going missing. Meikah is determined to do something about it before Rafe gets hurt. She's been warned they have to work within the law, that some of the members are nobles and without proof they can't pay for their crimes. Will they gain the proof needed before more innocent vampires go missing or is the society too well organised and impossible to catch?

*

This story was written by an Australian author using Australian spelling.

Name Pronunciation

Like many names there is more than one way to pronounce the following ones. These are the pronunciations used in this story.

Amiel (ah-meel)

Breena (bree-nah)

Cato (cay-toe)

Ena (en-ah)

Isha (ee-sha)

Kellan (kell-en)

Livia (liv-ee-ah)

Maksim (mack-sim)

Meikah (mee-cah)

Sarette (sah-ret)

Sirena (sigh-ren-ah)

Tertia (ter-sha)

Chapter One

Meikah trudged up the stairs of Fable, unbuckling her weapons as she went. How long would it take before she could do a simple spell? She was beginning to think it would take a lot longer than anyone had expected. Reaching the top of the stairs, she entered the hallway, walking towards the third door on the right. The room Kellan kept saying was hers. She'd stayed in it when they'd returned from the Arcton Mountains three nights ago. There'd been questions from Danton and the rest of the assassins to answer. The many questions hadn't surprised her. She would have had just as many if she'd been the one left behind.

The past two nights she'd stayed at home and her parents had barely spoken to her. When she'd arrived home two mornings ago they'd told her she was to go nowhere other than the Dark Blade Academy. That conversation hadn't been a pleasant experience and she'd almost been happy to go to the academy. She hadn't felt the same after a torturous day there and instead of going home, like she'd been told, she'd come here to Fable.

Yesterday and today she'd slipped out of her bedroom window the moment her parents had left to visit friends. Danton had organised for a sorcerer to train her. One who owed him a favour. An extremely experienced sorcerer. Not that it seemed to matter with how little she was learning. It was probably a good thing she wore a full face mask so he didn't know who he trained. There were already more than enough negative rumours circulating about her.

Swinging open the door, she took one step into the room before freezing, her gaze fixed on the bed. Or more accurately, what was laid out on the bed. A dress finer than she'd ever owned. An evening gown made of burgundy silk.

"What do you think?"

She spun to face Kellan. She hadn't heard him. "What's it for?" His broad shoulders filled the doorway and his black hair was tied at the nape of his neck. She found herself looking into his dark brown eyes trying to figure out what he was up to.

"It's for you to wear of course." Kellan grinned.

"For me?" Frowning, she placed the weapons she carried on the chest of drawers that was near the bed, careful not to knock over the flickering candle. "It might not fit me." Those hadn't been the words she'd planned to speak. It had been a demand as to why there was an evening gown on the bed.

"It will. I copied down your measurements before Danton sent them off to have your battle outfit made." Kellan gestured towards the gown. "Are you going to try it on?"

She removed her mask and dropped it on the chest of drawers next to the weapons. "The measurements were only taken two days ago. And not until the afternoon. How can a gown have been made that quickly?" She'd heard Sirena and Harlen's complaints often enough when they were waiting for new outfits, to wear to important functions, to know that seamstresses weren't that quick. Although with the outfits her grandparents already owned, they didn't really need more.

"It was meant to be for another customer, but the colour didn't suit. They should have listened to the seamstress to start with. Only a few alterations had to be made so it could fit you. I thought it would go well with your hair."

She half raised a hand to her dark brown hair that was in a plait down her back. "I can't-"

Kellan interrupted her. "Tonight. I have four invitations from Lady Eris for this evening's entertainment. It's a dance."

"Four?" She'd begun to think it was the event they were to attend together with the way he kept avoiding her question. The one in payment of the bet she'd lost.

"The rumours are starting to die down so it's time to ensure that doesn't happen. Try the gown on." Kellan closed the door, remaining in the hallway.

She looked from the door to the bed. How was this meant to create rumours? She slowly shook her head, crossing the short distance to the bed to pick up the gown. Her gaze remained on the item revealed underneath. A dagger in a thigh sheath. Dropping the gown on the bed, she picked up the weapon, drawing the dagger from the sheath. It was a simple weapon, sharp and well taken care of. What was he planning now? She opened the door to find he leaned against the wall opposite, his arms crossed over his chest. "What are you up to?"

Kellan stepped away from the wall, uncrossing his arms. "I already told you. Keeping the gossips busy." He gestured towards the gown on the bed. "Try that on and see if it fits." He grinned. "When we find that out, then I can tell you what the plan is."

She stared at him for a moment, catching a glimpse of mist forming in his brown eyes. Whatever it was, she doubted it would be simple. None of his plans ever were. "Just because you come up with a plan, doesn't mean we're going to follow it." She closed the door, facing the bed again and slipping the dagger back into the sheath. It didn't take long to strip off her clothes and pull on the gown. The garment fit perfectly. She ran her hands over the material. It was too fine a garment to be part of one of Kellan's schemes. It had probably cost a small fortune. And she was grounded. At the rate things were going, she'd be grounded for the rest of her life. Her gaze was drawn to the bed. Unless of course she was thrown out of home. She was beginning to think that was a distinct possibility. Picking up the sheathed dagger, she opened the door. "How is this involved in your plan?"

"You'll need to wear it." He grinned again, mist rising in his eyes. "You'll know when to draw it. And the line you need to speak is that we need to fight you, not each other."

Meikah frowned. "That doesn't make any sense."

"It will. Eventually." Kellan looked her up and down. "I knew it would look good on you."

She backed away, not liking the look in his eyes. They were full of mischief and admiration. It was the mischief that concerned her. "I can't go. Have you forgotten I'm grounded?"

"I've already accepted for you. Lady Eris suggested you might like to bring along a relative, to chaperone you, when she heard who my two guests were. Which is how I ended up with a fourth invitation rather than the initial three I requested."

Meikah closed her eyes and drew in a long, slow breath. Opening her eyes made no difference. Kellan continued to stand in front of her with the same look in his eyes. "Are you trying to get me thrown out of home?"

"I suggest you bring Isha with you. She's the one less likely to be upset by tonight's events," Kellan said. "I can send a carriage to collect the two of you at seven this evening. Isha first."

"Are you listening to me?" Meikah pointed the sheathed dagger at him. "I am not going to cause a fuss at Lady Eris' dance." She could imagine how much that'd upset Harlen. He'd lecture her for hours. Particularly if her actions caused Lady Eris to never invite a member of her family to one of her events again. Harlen had been trying to gain an invitation for years.

Kellan stepped close, taking the dagger from her. "Rafe agreed to help. You know we have to keep the rumours flying. And it's either the ones we come up with or the ones about you being a necromancer."

She sighed heavily. "But Lady Eris?" The woman was terrifying. She'd seen Harlen agree with her on more than one occasion when she knew he would have preferred to disagree. "None of my family will ever be invited to one of her events ever again. That would probably be enough to cause my grandparents to disown me."

"You might be surprised. She likes having her events talked about as much or more than the rest of the nobles."

She took the dagger from him. "You better not get me run out of town."

"But I can get you thrown out of home?"

"No. Neither." She closed the door more firmly than she'd planned. Turning her back on the door, she leaned against it. This was crazy. She looked down at the dagger she held. Whatever Kellan had planned, it was likely to draw the attention of every single guest at the dance. She was unaccustomed to that much attention. Pushing away from the door, she changed out of the gown and opened the door again to find Kellan still in the hallway.

"Would you like me to walk you home?"

"I can find my own way." She looked at the garment and sheathed dagger. "I'll need something to carry them in."

Chapter Two

Once Kellan had found her a satchel to put the neatly folded gown in, along with the weapon, she headed to her grandmother's home instead of her own. It was past time she visited Isha. She'd been meaning to ever since she'd returned from the Arcton Mountains. Hurrying to the outskirts of town, she tried not to think about how late the day was growing. If she didn't arrive home before her parents, she doubted even the thought of her attending one of Lady Eris' events would convince them to let her go out this evening.

Isha opened her front door, smiling at the sight of Meikah. The smile faded as quickly as it had begun. "What's wrong, Meikie? Come inside and tell me."

She'd barely stepped inside before Isha's arms were wrapped around her. She returned the hug. "I think I'm going to be in more trouble after tonight,

Grandmother Isha." She drew back. "And I need you to help me."

"In trouble with who?"

"With Grandfather Harlen."

Isha grinned. "Well, in that case, count me in. Come and tell me all about it." She closed the door, drawing Meikah further inside the small house. "Did you want something to eat first?"

Meikah shook her head. "I can't stay long. I need to be home before my parents. Kellan has an invitation for me to attend lady Eris' dance tonight. Along with a family member to chaperone me. Apart from that, I really can't tell you much about the mischief he's planning."

Isha chuckled. "Knowing that boy, it will keep the gossips' tongues wagging for days to come."

Meikah sighed. "That's what I'm worried about."

Isha examined her carefully. "Is there a reason why you feel compelled to join him in his latest mischief?"

"Some rumours are preferable to others." She smiled wryly. "And he does seem to be a master at creating rumours."

"That he does. I'd say you've involved an expert. What do you need me to do, Meikie?"

The childhood name calmed her, reminding her she wasn't the same person she'd been only a week ago. A lot had happened in a very little time. "A carriage will arrive to pick you up at seven this evening. I need you to convince my parents I should go with you."

"I don't think that's going to be a difficult task. The moment they hear Lady Eris, the pair of them will be wanting to join us."

"I can only bring along one family member."

Isha chuckled. "I'm sure by morning they'll be relieved it was me, and not them, you took with you."

Meikah winced. "I've got a feeling it will be tonight they feel that way." She glanced at the door. "I should probably go so I can be home before they are."

Isha opened the door. "You know you're always welcome here. If things become too unbearable at home, there'll always be a bed here for you. Maksim would say the same."

Meikah threw her arms around Isha. "I know."

Isha hugged her equally tight. "I'm proud of you, Meikie. Your grandfather would be too. You keep holding your head high and don't let any of those rumours bother you. Or pay any heed to the rest of the family. What you're doing is better than their idea of hiding you away in the hope that everyone forgets. Society's memory is far longer than most people appreciate."

All she could do was smile even though she wanted to thank her grandmother. There was a lump in her throat which seemed unusually tight. Nodding, she pulled away. With another smile, she hurried down the road. She glanced over her shoulder to see Isha watched her leave. She waved, smiling again when her grandmother waved back.

She barely managed to arrive home in time, clambering through the window and laying the gown out on the bed in the hope that the few creases it had gained would fall out. Rather than risk someone coming into her room and spot the dress, she headed downstairs to endure the disappointed looks and silence from her parents.

When she would have normally joined them at the table for dinner, she excused herself, saying she needed to use the bathroom. Instead, she made her way upstairs and changed into the gown, reaching the front door in time to let Isha in. Her hand brushed across the weapon in the thigh sheath, thankfully not noticeable through the material of the gown. She wasn't accustomed to wearing such a weapon. Normally she had a sword at her side. And lately a dagger too. Neither were hidden when she wore them.

Isha entered the house. "I take it they're sitting down to dinner?"

Meikah nodded, unaccustomed to seeing Isha in such fancy clothes.

"You can wait here if you want." Isha patted Meikah on the arm before she strode through the house.

Meikah planned to remain by the door. When the expected raised voices couldn't be heard, she hurried to the dining table to see the shocked expressions on her parents' faces.

Ena rose from the table, pointing at Meikah. "Her. She's been invited to the dance Lady Eris is holding tonight."

Isha slipped an arm around Meikah's shoulders. "Yes, we really should be going. I doubt she'd appreciate us arriving late."

Meikah walked beside Isha, surprised her parents remained silent. Although she'd never seen such expressions on their faces before. Not even when they'd learned she was a necromancer. Once in the carriage, she began to relax. "Did they say anything?" Maybe they'd spoken too quietly for her to have heard from where she'd waited by the front door.

Isha chuckled. "Give them time to get over the shock and I'm sure they'll have plenty to say."

Meikah nodded. Once they heard the new rumours they'd have too much to say. She really wasn't looking forward to another lecture from Harlen. Her grandfather was a master at giving lectures. Although her father was getting better at it with all the practice he'd had lately.

When the carriage drew to a stop in front of Lady Eris' mansion, the door was opened and Kellan held out his hand to help first Isha and then Meikah exit. "You both look lovely this evening."

Meikah looked Kellan up and down. He was dressed in evening wear and it certainly suited him. Movement behind him drew her attention and she noticed Rafe was also dressed in evening wear. Both of them wore dark trousers and long sleeve shirts with embroidery decorating the cuffs. They also wore swords at their sides in decorative scabbards. "The two of you look good."

Rafe stepped forward and held out an arm. "Allow me to escort you inside."

Meikah looked from Rafe to Kellan, placing a hand on Rafe's arm. "Thank you." Was this part of their plan? She glanced over her shoulder to see Kellan escorted Isha.

Inside Kellan introduced her to numerous people, including Lady Eris. The woman looked her up and down. "I've heard a lot about you."

Meikah wasn't sure if she wanted to know if that was good or bad. She smiled, nodded then moved along so the next guest could greet their host. Isha joined the rest of the chaperones gossiping around the edges of the ballroom and Meikah took turns dancing with Rafe and Kellan. After about an hour, Kellan and Rafe escorted the two of them to supper which was held in a room adjoining the ballroom.

Helping herself to the buffet, she began to relax. Maybe whatever Kellan had planned wouldn't be so bad. After all, she'd already heard people talking about the fact she'd only danced with the two of them and no other partners. Finished eating she placed her hand on Kellan's arm, that he offered, and started back to the ballroom.

As they approached the doorway, Cato stepped through it and into the supper room, freezing when he caught sight of her. "Meikah."

Chapter Three

Meikah wanted to ignore Cato. Wanted to look him up and down like he was some disgusting creature she'd stumbled across, then keep walking. But did she really want to make a scene? Especially when other guests had turned towards them when Cato had spoken. She couldn't resist looking him up and down, even though she didn't do it in a way to suggest he was something she'd found hiding under a rock. He didn't look anywhere near as good as Kellan and Rafe in his evening wear. "Cato."

"You know Lady Eris?" Cato's gaze darted away several times.

Anger rushed through her. She was not the one who'd tried to act like she hadn't known him because of some necromancer rumours. Even though the rumours had been true. "So it would seem." She turned to Kellan. "I believe you owe me a dance."

Rafe stepped forward, holding out his hand. "No, that would be me."

She placed her hand in his, gratefully walking beside him into the ballroom, not bothering to say goodbye to Cato. She smiled up at him as he spun her around the dance floor, speaking softly, knowing he would hear. "Thank you."

Rafe grinned, nodding slightly.

When the song ended, he led her to Kellan, placing her hand on Kellan's arm. She walked beside Kellan back onto the dance floor, catching a glimpse of Cato amongst the other well dressed guests. He watched her, looking away when he saw her attention on him. Once that would have bothered her far more than it currently did. Now, it only annoyed her.

"Should I be offended that you waste your attention on another when you're dancing with me?"

She grinned up at Kellan. "I don't know. Why don't you tell me?"

Kellan chuckled, spinning her across the floor amongst the dancing couples. When the song ended, he remained on the floor, his arms around her.

She glanced at Rafe at the side of the room. "Why are we standing here?"

Kellan grinned, not answering.

"Kellan." There was a warning note in her voice.

What was he planning? She'd started to think she'd figured it out. She had a bad feeling she hadn't been close.

Rafe reached them, holding out his hand to Meikah. "I believe this is my dance."

The music started and Meikah began to reach for Rafe's hand.

Kellan captured her hand before she could make contact. "That was a shorter song. This dance should be mine too."

Rafe shrugged. "Sometimes you're unlucky. This is my dance." Again he held his hand out to Meikah. Around them couples began to dance, giving them a wide berth.

Kellan pushed Rafe's hand down. "That is not acceptable."

Rafe's eyes narrowed. "Neither is you trying to take my dance."

Kellan drew his sword. "Winner has the next dance."

Rafe also drew his sword, a murmur going through the crowd, those dancing around them moving further away. Some of them stopped to watch. "Winner has the rest of the dances for the evening."

Meikah looked from one to the other. Surely this wasn't the moment Kellan had expected her to draw the dagger and demand they fight her. They had swords. How fair was that?

Kellan nodded. "I like that plan better. Winner has the rest of the dances for the evening."

Meikah tried not to pay any attention to the comments already being made. She didn't like where this plan was going. "What if I don't want to dance with either of you for the rest of this evening?"

Kellan grinned, sharing a look with Rafe before returning his attention to Meikah. "Why would you want to dance with anyone else?"

Meikah wished she could ignore the looks, giggles and laughter directed towards her. What was he trying to do? Make her the joke? She caught sight of Cato again, a smirk on his face. She lifted her chin, trying not to think about the time when a couple of words from Cato had made her drop her sword. It might have only been two weeks ago, but after all she'd faced there was no chance she'd ever do that again. "Sometimes you think a little too much of yourself, Kellan." Drawing up the side of her dress, she drew her dagger as quickly as possible, letting the skirt of the dress fall back into place. "And it's not each other you should be fighting if you want to dance with me. It's me you should fight."

Kellan nodded to her dagger. "That hardly seems a

fair fight when you have a dagger and we each have a sword."

Rafe held his sword out to Meikah, hilt first. "Allow me to offer my sword. Kellan is right. It wouldn't be fair if we had a sword and you a dagger. Kellan can go first. I'll fight the winner."

Meikah shifted the dagger to her left hand and took the sword from Rafe, surprised the balance suited her. Had they planned even this aspect of the evening? She faced Kellan, who drew a dagger before attacking with both weapons. It felt more like a practice session than an actual fight to win. She grinned. And it had been days since she'd had an actual practice session with a sword. They wanted her to practice her magic, but she was beginning to think this was what she needed to focus on. She was getting nowhere with magic. She met each of Kellan's attacks and got in several of her own, driving him backwards.

"What is going on here?" Lady Eris' voice rang out over the many shocked comments and rumours already beginning.

Kellan stepped back, lowering his sword and dagger. "Lady Eris." He bowed to her. "We've found the perfect method for when a lady cannot decide which gentleman she wishes to dance with."

Meikah lowered her weapons, trying to ignore the

sinking sensation in her stomach. She wanted to stare at the floor when she saw the woman's expression. Somehow, she managed to hold her gaze. "Or a way to completely avoid dancing with that particular gentleman." She eyed Kellan up and down before returning her attention to Lady Eris. She would have words with Kellan later.

"Do you think you can beat Kellan in a sword fight?" Lady Eris' tone clearly told everyone how little she thought that was possible.

Meikah continued to hold her gaze. She didn't know if she could beat him, but she wasn't about to admit defeat before she'd met the challenge. "Yes."

"Really?" Once more Lady Eris' tone was filled with disbelief.

Meikah took a deep breath. Why hadn't Kellan told her exactly what the plan was? She would have told him to come up with another one. "Would you like me to show you?" Behind her, she heard a ripple of laughter. Some of it sounded nervous, but she was almost certain a few were amused.

Lady Eris held her gaze for nearly a minute, silence falling, broken only by several people clearing their throat and one person giving a cut off, nervous laugh. "Yes. Not in here though. In the grounds. I will not have my ballroom damaged." She gestured towards the nearby doors that led into the well-lit gardens.

Meikah stood where she was for a moment, not sure she'd heard correctly. Lady Eris wanted to see her fight? With a nod, she headed for the door, Kellan reaching them before her and opening them, bowing her through. She ignored the glint of humour in his eyes, striding into the gardens. This was as crazy as the flagpole incident. Well, maybe not. At least the Duke wasn't involved this time. She caught sight of Cato again. The amusement on his face made her narrow her eyes. She couldn't believe he'd once caused her to drop her sword due to his attention. Now she would have preferred to run him through with it.

"The centre of attention, as always, Kellan."

Chapter Four

Hearing the familiar voice, Meikah's eyes widened as she slowly turned. She almost closed her eyes when she found the Duke had followed them into the gardens, a goblet in one hand. She lost all power of speech and couldn't remember if she was to bow or curtsey.

Kellan grinned. "Your Grace. How lovely to see you. Is the Duchess with you this evening? This would be the perfect event for her to wear her new scarf."

Rafe moved closer to Meikah, sharing a look with her.

She didn't blame Rafe. It seemed there was little Kellan wouldn't dare. She finally managed to curtsey to the Duke. "Your Grace."

He inclined his head. "Meikah, isn't it?"

"Yes, Your Grace."

The Duke looked at Rafe. "And Rafe."

"Yes, Your Grace." Rafe bowed.

"Considerate of you to lend a lady your sword," the Duke said.

"Ah, yes, Your Grace."

The Duke gestured towards a clear spot in the gardens, plenty of lanterns around the area to light it up well. His gaze remained on Meikah. "Don't let me keep you. I believe you promised Lady Eris that you'd teach this young man a lesson." He glanced at Kellan. "Probably a long overdue event."

She had? Meikah looked from the Duke to Kellan and back again, her grip tightening on her weapons. What would happen if lightning crawled along the blade of her sword? She'd been practicing calling it when needed and not having it come when she didn't want it to, but she was nowhere near perfect. "Yes, Your Grace." She tried to swallow, her throat feeling like it was closing in on itself.

Kellan strode to the area the Duke had indicated, facing Meikah with a grin, his sword and dagger held ready. "I don't know, Meikah. Being the one to claim all your dances for the evening is a fairly big incentive for me to win."

Her shoulders straightened and she strode towards him, her breath coming easier, particularly when she caught sight of Cato laughing at Kellan's comment. "Likewise."

"The thought of dancing with me is an incentive for you to lose?" Kellan asked.

"No." She raised her sword, the dagger gripped tightly in her left hand. "The thought of dancing with only you all evening is an incentive for me to win." She attacked, driving him back.

Kellan returned her attacks, nearly getting past her defences. "Then that should make this an interesting match."

She focused on Kellan, the crowd around them fading into the background. Normally it wasn't good to focus on one thing to the exclusion of all else in a fight, but she trusted Rafe to watch over them and make sure no harm came to either of them. They seemed more evenly matched than usual and Meikah's gaze narrowed when she realised that Kellan met her attacks rather than made any attempts to get past them. It was barely noticeable, but she'd seen him fight enough times to realise. She lunged, trying to throw him off balance.

Kellan grinned. "I feel like our evening of endless dancing has already begun."

A ripple of laughter went through the crowd. Meikah caught a glimpse of the Duke's grin before she blocked out the crowd again to focus on besting Kellan. "Then I suggest you make the most of it since this is all the dancing you'll be doing with me for the rest of the evening." More laughter rippled through the crowd.

"Your words feel sharper than the sword you wield," Kellan protested.

"I've heard the truth has a tendency to hurt." Meikah attacked rapidly, wanting to disarm him. She blocked his dagger with hers, the skirt of her gown slowing some of her movements. No wonder she preferred trousers. Somehow or other, she wasn't sure if she managed it or Kellan allowed it to happen, his sword was knocked from his hand to spin through the air.

Rafe dashed towards the sword, catching it before it could hit the ground in front of the Duke. With a bow to the Duke, he turned to Meikah with a grin. "I believe I am to face the winner."

Meikah lowered her sword. There was no way she could beat a vampire. Not with how fast he moved. And none of the guests would believe it if she did win. "I have no objections to dancing with you this evening." She glanced around the crowd, surprised to see several of the guests were smiling at her in approval, particularly the older women and the young men around her age. She held Rafe's sword out to him. "If you have no objections."

Rafe took the sword from her. "I certainly have no objections." He sheathed his sword, holding Kellan's out to him.

Kellan took the sword, sheathing it. "Maybe Isha will console me by allowing me to escort her to the dance floor." Kellan grinned at the elderly woman who was in the crowd not far from the Duke. "And possibly tell me some childhood stories about Meikah."

Isha chuckled. "I fear you'll have to do better than that."

The Duke stepped forward. "Allow me to congratulate you on your victory." He placed a hand on Meikah's shoulder and leaned forward to kiss her cheek, speaking softly. "Let my brother know the Society Against Vampires have recruited some of the nobility and are being welcomed at many of the most elite functions. They could also be the ones watching my every move." He stepped back. "It's always good to see Kellan meet his match." He chuckled. "I'm afraid it doesn't happen near often enough."

"Thank you, Your Grace." Meikah didn't know if he expected her to leave now or remain until the guests started to depart. How important was it to get the message to Danton?

Several people came up to Meikah, congratulating her on the win and it began to feel awkward holding the dagger. Nor did she want to return it to the thigh sheath. Putting it away wasn't going to be as easy as taking it out. Excusing herself, she made her way to the bathroom. After sheathing the dagger, she made use of the opulent facilities before stepping outside, running into a young man she'd seen watching the fight.

"I'm terribly sorry." The young man bowed. "I noticed the Duke appeared quite taken with you. Are you a personal friend of his?" His evening wear was cut to fit his muscular frame and his blue eyes looked her up and down, his light brown hair kept exceptionally short. As short as that of a soldier.

She didn't know what to say. If she said no, would that make his actions seem out of character to whoever was watching? She smiled. "I don't believe we've met before." She held out her hand. "I'm Meikah."

He took her hand, raising it to his lips. "Delighted. I'm Tobin. My family arrived a few days ago. We're staying with Lord Barnet. My father and myself.

Maybe you've heard of my father. Hemmet. He's been to Dreyton before."

Her smile remained in place while she struggled to think of a way to keep the conversation away from the Duke. The name Hemmet was as unfamiliar to her as Tobin. "Lord Barnet has never struck me as being overly sociable." Harlen had tried to call on him a few times, but the man was never at home. Yet as far as anyone knew, he never went out either. At least not since his son disappeared a decade ago.

"We're staying with him at his invitation," Tobin said.

Once again she was at a loss for words.

"Does the Duke invite you to all his gatherings?" Tobin asked.

Thinking it would have been a terrible idea to tell him she'd never been to any of the Duke's gatherings, Meikah was relieved to see Rafe stride towards them. She smiled at him in greeting.

Tobin turned in time to see the smile Rafe gave her. "You are friends?" His tone of voice clearly indicated that he expected her to say no.

"Yes. We're good friends."

"He's a vampire." Tobin looked Rafe up and down, a look of disgust on his face.

Rafe's smile faded. He barely gave Tobin a glance,

focusing his attention on Meikah. "Your grandmother is tired and would like to go home. Kellan wore her out dancing." Rafe grinned. "It wouldn't surprise me if it was deliberate on his part."

Meikah chuckled. "It wouldn't surprise me either." She took a step towards Rafe, looking at Tobin. "I better go."

Tobin inclined his head, striding away, a last glare directed at Rafe.

Meikah rested a hand on Rafe's arm. "Are you all right?" She glanced in the direction Tobin had taken.

Rafe took her hand from his arm, holding it in his. "There are always those who dislike vampires. Some have reason to."

It reminded her of how she'd been judged when people learned she was a necromancer. "He doesn't know you."

Rafe shrugged. "Kellan has already said goodbye to our host while I took your grandmother out to the carriage." He led the way through the house.

"Is Grandmother Isha all right? She didn't overdo things, did she?" She couldn't think of a time when Isha had begged off anything due to exhaustion. Was she ill?

"We'll be at the carriage shortly and you'll be able to see she's fine," Rafe said.

Chapter Five

Stepping outside, Meikah nearly ran into Cato. She stepped around him, pulling away from Rafe as she picked up her pace, heading for the carriage that wasn't far from her.

"Meikah, wait." Cato hurried after her.

She was tempted to keep walking. Stopping, she faced him. "I'm in a hurry. I need to see Grandmother Isha home."

Cato shifted from one foot to the other, a glance at Rafe. "I never expected to see you here. Not after the rumours."

Meikah knew exactly which rumours he was referring to, but bringing them up wouldn't help her endeavour of making people forget them. "People did warn me that hanging around Kellan would probably get me involved in some of his pranks." She shrugged. "I'm not about to desert a friend over a few rumours."

"Ahh… I mean, the other ones." Cato glanced away, looking at the ground rather than meeting Meikah's gaze.

Kellan came out of the carriage to stand beside Meikah. "There's absolutely no truth in them." He slowly shook his head. "Sadly, she keeps turning me down."

Cato looked from one to the other several times. "Turning you down?"

"Yes." Kellan took Meikah's hand, raising it to his lips. "But I have hope." He smiled at Cato. "If you will excuse us." He kept hold of Meikah's hand, helping her into the carriage when they reached it.

Meikah waited until they were seated, and the carriage had moved off, before she spoke to Kellan. "What were you thinking? Now he probably thinks you proposed or something."

Kellan chuckled, glancing at Isha before meeting Meikah's gaze. "What does it matter? You didn't want to talk to him."

"No, but-" She broke off, having no idea what she could say without letting Isha know something she shouldn't.

"You're welcome then." Kellan turned to Isha. "Sorry to end the evening so abruptly. And thank you for playing along."

Meikah frowned, looking from Isha to Kellan. "What do you mean? Playing along."

Kellan nodded to Rafe. "There were a few attending tonight who weren't happy to have a vampire there. I thought we should leave before things became ugly."

"Are you all right, Rafe?" Meikah checked him over in the limited light, that entered the windows of the carriage, from the lampposts they passed.

Kellan spoke before Rafe had a chance. "How did you find your first dance, Meikah?"

Her gaze momentarily rested on his sword. "Not quite what I was expecting."

Kellan chuckled. "The unexpected is always more interesting." The carriage pulled up and Kellan opened the door, helping Isha out. "Thank you for accepting the invitation this evening."

"It has certainly been entertaining." Isha turned to Meikah who joined them in front of the cottage. "Are you sure you don't want me to come home with you? I daresay by now your parents will have heard about this evening's antics."

Meikah hugged Isha. "I'll be fine." She wanted to find out what had happened to Rafe that had made Kellan call an end to the night. She doubted he'd discuss it in front of Isha. "Thank you for attending the dance with me."

When they were back in the carriage and Meikah tried to speak, Kellan interrupted her. "We'll be at Fable shortly. It can wait until then."

"But I want to know what-" Meikah started to say.

Kellan, who'd been sitting opposite her shifted over to sit beside her. He tilted his head close to hers. "Have you forgotten the coachman?"

Meikah frowned as she tried to figure out what was going on. She leaned close to him so she could whisper in his ear. "We didn't leave because of Rafe, did we?"

"Not at all." Kellan grinned.

She returned his grin, glancing at Rafe. Danton had another task for them? She desperately wanted to ask, but Kellan was right. This wasn't something they could speak about while the coachman might hear. The moment the carriage pulled up in front of Fable, Meikah hurried out of it before Kellan had the chance to help her. Entering the front door of Fable, she was disappointed to find the bookshop empty. She'd half expected all of them in there waiting to talk about what was going on.

Rafe joined her. "They're at the back of the shop."

"What happened?" Meikah asked. "What was the message?"

Rafe shrugged. "Shade arrived, waited until we saw him, nodded once then left. Kellan told me that was the signal that Danton needed to speak to us."

Kellan entered the bookshop. "It is."

Meikah glanced at the door. "What took you so long?"

"I had to tell the coachman I wouldn't need him again this evening." Kellan strode towards the counter and the curtained doorway behind it.

Meikah hurried after him. "I'm not wearing footwear suited to walking."

"There'll be a pair of boots you can borrow." Kellan stepped through the doorway.

"And exactly how will I explain that to my parents?" Meikah followed him through the small hallway and into the kitchen.

Kellan grinned. "I'm sure you'll think of something." He joined the group at the table.

Sighing, Meikah looked at Danton, Livia and Shade who were seated at the table, taking the bowls of soup Mace handed them. Amiel stood nearby, glaring at Shade. She wasn't tempted to ask what Shade had said to annoy the necromancer spirit this time.

Mace smiled at Meikah. "Are you hungry too?"

Nodding, she sat at the table, thanking him for the bowl of soup he handed her before serving Kellan. She looked towards Danton. "The Duke asked me to give you a message. He believes the Society Against Vampires might be watching him and they have recruited some of the nobility. They're also being invited to elite functions."

"When did he tell you that?" Kellan asked.

"After she defeated you." Rafe joined them at the table, no bowl of soup in front of him.

Kellan grinned. "Are you sure she defeated me?"

Before Meikah could ask if he'd let her win, Danton spoke.

"One of you need to keep an eye on my brother and figure out who is watching him. Someone else needs to infiltrate the Society Against Vampires."

"I can watch the Duke," Shade said.

Livia linked her fingers through Shade's. "We can watch the Duke."

"Who is interested in infiltrating SAV?" Danton asked. "Someone needs to get close to Lord Hemmet, a guest of Lord Barnet's. There are rumours that he's a high ranking member of SAV."

Finished her soup, Meikah set the spoon down. "That counts me out. His son knows I'm friends with a vampire." She glanced at Rafe, smiling to let him know she was glad to be friends with him.

Danton slowly nodded. "Maybe not."

Kellan grinned. "Being betrayed by a vampire after being their friend could be a quick way into SAV."

"Rafe would never betray me," Meikah exclaimed.

"Of course he wouldn't," Kellan said. "But they don't know that."

"What if it wasn't Rafe, but a vampire who is a stranger?" Livia asked.

Suggestions went back and forth as they argued them out until Amiel glared at them. "It's a wonder anything gets done around here." He pointed a finger at Danton. "You're meant to run things. Tell them what to do and be done with it."

Danton didn't look in the least bothered by Amiel's outburst. "I value their suggestions."

"You value mine the most, don't you?" Kellan asked.

"Of course he doesn't," Mace said. "It's mine he values most."

Amiel threw his hands up. "I'll check the vampire isn't getting into anything. At least one of us should be doing something useful." He strode towards the hallway.

Chapter Six

Meikah stared in the direction Amiel had taken. "Vampire?"

Danton nodded. "A vampire called earlier saying her husband has been missing since the night SAV arrived. No one has been willing to help her find him. She's sleeping in the basement. The poor woman is exhausted. She's been searching for him every night and can barely sleep during the day as she tries to think of where she hasn't looked. I'll see that she gets home safely before morning."

"Befriending Tobin might be a way to get to his father," Rafe suggested. "I can follow him and see where he goes and who he knows."

Danton shook his head. "Until SAV are dealt with, none of you are to go anywhere alone of an evening, nor enter unpopulated areas by yourself during the day. If my little brother is being watched too closely for him to get a message to me then they're highly organised."

"Your little brother." Meikah stared at Danton. He was the oldest? "You should have been the Duke?"

Danton chuckled. "Do you think the rumours would have ended if I'd not abdicated?"

Her problems seemed insignificant. Being accused a necromancer had caused minor inconveniences in comparison. "I'm sorry."

"Don't be. I think my brother ended up with the worst part of the deal. Being an Assassin Of The Dead is a lot more interesting than being the Duke." Danton turned to Mace. "Can you shadow Tobin along with Kellan?"

Mace nodded. "Should we send to the capital? There aren't going to be enough of us to watch everyone."

"They have their own problems to deal with." Danton rose from the table. "When we have more information, we'll figure out our next step. It might be that we need to ask for more help, but we'll see what we can do first." He turned to Kellan. "You and Rafe take Meikah home before her parents are wondering where she is. Lady Eris' party has probably started to finish by now." He glanced around the table. "I know it will reduce the amount of time each of you has available for shadowing Tobin and my brother, but I was serious when I said I don't want any of you working alone. SAV are dangerous."

"Then why doesn't the Duke do something about them?" Meikah stood up, pushing the chair back under the table.

"He can only work within the law and they're good at hiding their crimes," Danton said. "Without proof, he can't do anything."

Amiel entered the kitchen. "The vampire woman is being dramatic. Saying there's no point in living when her husband is dead. That forever is only worth having if you have someone at your side to share it."

"Show some compassion, Amiel." Danton strode to the hallway, pausing at the entrance to look over his shoulder. "Don't get caught." He entered the shadowy hallway.

Meikah grinned at the familiar words, her grin fading as she thought about how dangerous Dreyton had become for Rafe. She didn't want anything to happen to him.

Mace headed for the hallway. "You'd think Danton would know by now that you have no compassion." He glanced at Amiel as he walked past him.

The spirit followed Mace from the kitchen. "And you have too much. Half the time I can't believe you're the descendant of mine that shows the most promise as a necromancer. When are you going to realise you're wasting your talents here?"

Meikah didn't hear Mace's answer, he was already out of sight and hearing. She turned to Kellan. "You mentioned boots earlier."

Kellan nodded. "Let me get changed into something suitable and once Rafe and I have returned you home, we'll help Mace."

She started to protest, especially when Shade and Livia headed out the back door. She wanted to help. Going home was the last thing she wanted to do. She thought of the room upstairs that Kellan kept saying belonged to her. If she lived here, she wouldn't have to sneak out or come up with excuses about what she was doing. But would that mean her family would have nothing more to do with her? She didn't want to lose her family.

"I better get changed too." Rafe followed Kellan.

Meikah was left alone in the kitchen. She stared wistfully at the back door Shade and Livia had closed behind them. She didn't want to be left out of everything. She was an Assassin Of The Dead. Images of her family came to mind. Harlen would probably demand her existence be forgotten, but what about the rest of them? Isha and Maksim would always be there for her. Would her parents and sister?

"Are you all right?"

Meikah spun to face Rafe who was at the hallway entrance, dressed in a navy outfit suitable for blending into the shadows. Not that he had any problems blending in no matter what he wore. He carried the full face mask he'd use for following Tobin. She had no idea what to tell him.

Rafe crossed the space between them in a blur, taking hold of her hand. "Meikah?"

"I want to help, but…" Her voice trailed off.

"You will help. Just not this morning."

"It's after midnight already?" It always surprised her that he could tell what time of night it was.

Rafe inclined his head. "Kellan and Mace are coming down the stairs. Shall we meet them in the shop?" He continued to hold her hand.

Her gaze was drawn to her hand clasped in his. Yet one more thing she had no idea about what decision she should make. She drew her hand from his. "All right."

When he entered the shop, wearing a similar outfit to Rafe's, Kellan held out a pair of boots to Meikah. "You can put your dancing slippers back on and we'll take the boots with us." He grinned. "No need to come up with a story to tell your parents."

She took the boots from him, looking around for somewhere to sit while she put them on. When Rafe lifted her onto the counter, she started to protest, breaking off once she was seated. "Thank you." It wasn't like there was anywhere else she could sit.

The walk to her place was silent and they avoided the pools of light cast by the lampposts. There were very few people out at this hour of the night and only a single carriage rumbled past them, heading away from the centre of town. Meikah strode between Rafe and Kellan, Mace ahead of them. "Everything seems normal. It's hard to believe anything is wrong."

Kellan slung an arm around her shoulders. "There's always someone or something that needs to be dealt with. And if most people don't realise that, then we've done our job well. We don't only protect our town against necromancers and the dead they raise. We take care of anything the town guard or the Duke's men can't take care of."

Again they fell silent, not speaking until they'd reached Meikah's home. She looked around for somewhere to sit, making do with Kellan and Rafe supporting her. "Thank you." It was easier to put on slippers than boots.

"What are you thanking us for?" Kellan asked. "Walking you home or creating a few more rumours about you?"

Meikah chuckled. "I'm not sure I should be thanking you for tonight's rumours."

"You will." Kellan grinned. "You'll see. Before you know it, no one will ever believe the necromancer ones."

Meikah looked at each of them in the limited light. She didn't want to go home. She wanted to join them in seeing what Tobin was up to. But her parents were expecting her. "Goodnight." She hurried the rest of the distance to her front door, glancing over her shoulder as she reached it. None of them were in view, but she supposed that didn't mean they'd left the area yet. Trying the door handle, she found it locked. Sighing, she knocked. So much for sneaking inside and heading up to her bedroom before anyone noticed.

The door was flung open before she'd finished knocking. Heron glared down at her.

Chapter Seven

Meikah was tempted to take a step back from her father. She raised her chin, meeting his glare, trying to keep her magic under control. The anger filling her at his expression didn't help. "Are you going to let me in?"

"Are you trying to have your grandfather thrown off the Duke's council?"

She was half tempted to ask her father if she should see how the Duke felt about her behaviour. But she couldn't. "No."

"Then what am I meant to believe when you carry on like this? Did you think I wouldn't find out?" Heron demanded.

Of course she'd known he'd find out. "Are you going to let me inside?"

"One of my parents' friends were informing them of your behaviour before the dance had ended."

"Who told you?" She had a good idea who, but wanted to know for certain.

"My parents are shocked by your behaviour. They have suggested sending you to a school in the capital that specialises in teaching wayward children."

Fear rushed through her and she felt the magic rise. "Do you think you can make me go?"

Heron took a step back, a moment of fear in his expression before he ended his retreat. "You will do as you're told. You'll spend no more time with Kellan, even if he invites you to attend one of the Duke and Duchess' functions."

She wasn't about to let him stop her. That room at Fable was looking better by the minute. "I'm going to bed." She slipped past him.

"I haven't finished talking with you." Heron followed her up the stairs.

"I'm tired."

"That is too bad. Until you agree to stay away from Kellan, this conversation isn't over."

Why had she decided to come home? Reaching her door, she spun to face her father. "That isn't going to happen. I'm not about to turn my back on any of my friends."

"So you'll turn your back on your family instead," Heron demanded.

Sorrow washed through her, taking with it her anger. "What rumours have you heard about me lately?"

"The entire town is filled with rumours about you."

"I know, but what sort of rumours? Are any of them saying I'm a necromancer?" When her father didn't answer, she stepped into her room and closed the door, leaning against it in the dark.

Heron knocked on the door a moment later. "Open the door."

She stepped away from it before she spoke. "I'm getting changed." She didn't need to light a candle to slip out of her dress and get ready for bed. She'd used this bedroom her entire life. Knew every inch of it.

"Meikah." Heron knocked sharply on the door again.

Ignoring him, Meikah slipped into bed, pulling up the covers. Was that it? Was that why she refused to leave home? It was familiar. She'd certainly had to face a lot of changes lately. Maybe she needed to face one more. Anger raced through her. Why should she be forced to leave because they couldn't understand? It wasn't fair.

"Meikah." Heron banged loudly against the timber. "Open the door."

She rolled over onto her side, her father's voice

raised angrily, her mother's too soft to hear the words clearly. She didn't want to leave. Squeezing her eyes closed, she tried not to think about how it made her feel. One day she'd be ready to leave home and make her own way in the world, but she'd wanted it to be on her terms. Not because she was forced into it.

"Are you all right?" Kellan sat on the bed beside her.

Meikah opened her eyes, trying to see him in the darkness. "I thought you were meant to be watching Tobin." She kept her voice low. Not that her parents were likely to hear her with how loud her father was yelling, her mother's voice also growing louder.

"Want to help us?" Rafe asked.

"You're both in here?" Meikah asked.

"All of us," Mace said.

She was tired, but it'd be impossible to sleep with the noise in the hallway. Ena was likely to join in soon. "I'll meet you outside. I need to get dressed."

"Here." Kellan pressed a bundle of cloth into her hands. "Rafe went back for them."

"No one is meant to be out on their own," Meikah protested.

Rafe briefly rested a hand on her arm. "I'm too quick to be caught. We'll meet you outside. Now hurry. There aren't many hours left of the night."

As soon as the curtain twitched open, and the three of them had slipped through the window, Meikah got out of bed and dressed in the outfit they'd given her. She pulled on the full face mask as her parents continued to argue. Grabbing her sword and dagger, she slipped out the window once they were in place. She had no idea what to do. For now, she'd focus on the problems that could be solved. Making sure the Society Against Vampires couldn't come after Rafe.

It took them a couple of hours to find Tobin. They scoured the city for him, eventually finding him in a tavern with a bad reputation. They didn't find him until he was heading out the door with two companions and striding towards Lord Barnet's place. Following at a distance, they remained hidden the couple of times Tobin and his companions stopped to talk to other people. When Tobin's companions went their own way, Rafe wanted to split up and follow the two groups.

"It could be a trap," Kellan said.

"How could it be?" Rafe asked. "They haven't noticed us. Mace could come with me."

"We stay together," Meikah stated. "Danton said to stay together."

"None of us would be alone," Rafe said.

"You'll have to return to Fable before morning

and I'll probably have to go home before then too," Meikah said. "We stay together."

They continued to follow Tobin to Lord Barnet's, finding a position out the front where they could keep watch on the mansion.

Meikah drifted off to sleep, pressed between Kellan and Rafe. When Kellan moved slightly, it jarred her awake. She peered at the mansion. "Is he still inside?"

Mace, who was behind them, answered. "No one has entered or left the mansion. It's pretty quiet over there."

"That'll change soon. Once the servants get up and start getting organised for the coming day," Kellan said.

Meikah turned to Rafe. "It's nearly day?"

Rafe nodded. "I'll have to return to Fable shortly. Do you want me to walk you home?"

"Who will walk you the rest of the way?" Meikah asked.

Rafe smiled. "I'll be fine. No one would be able to keep up with me, let alone catch me over that short a distance."

"But-" Meikah started to say.

Rafe interrupted her. "I know they're out there. I won't take any unnecessary risks." He captured her hand. "You don't have to worry about me."

Meikah glanced at all of them. "You're not the only one I'm worried about." She drew her hand from Rafe's light grip, stumbling to her feet. "I should probably go home and get a couple of hours sleep. I have to attend the Dark Blade Academy today."

Kellan grinned. "We need to focus on getting you thrown out of there."

Meikah sighed. "At the rate I'm going, I'll be thrown out of home first."

Kellan chuckled. "Do you need me to come with you in case your parents have set the wards?"

She wasn't about to let him leave Mace here alone. "I'll figure something out." She said goodbye to Kellan and Mace, keeping to the shadows as her and Rafe wandered through the streets back to her place. Unlike earlier, the streets weren't as quiet. Tradesmen were about, making early morning deliveries and getting organised for the day. Meikah stopped in the shadows beside her house. "I'll see you this evening."

With a nod, Rafe slipped away into the shadows.

Chapter Eight

Meikah didn't bother looking for Rafe. As a vampire, he was more efficient at hiding than the assassins were. And she couldn't find them when they were hiding amongst the shadows. Pulling herself onto the roof, Meikah started to creep through her window, removing her mask, surprised to find the wards hadn't been set. She froze at a sound coming from the direction of her bed. She really needed to learn how to see in the dark.

"Meikah? Is that you?"

Meikah momentarily closed her eyes at hearing Breena's voice. "Yes." She finished climbing in the window, making her way over to the chest of drawers so she could light a candle. She left the mask beside the candle.

Breena sat up, blinking in the flickering light,

having been stretched out on top of the bedcovers. "Where have you been?"

Meikah shrugged. There wasn't anything she could tell her mother.

Breena crossed the space between them. "It's not safe wandering the streets alone. And where did you get that outfit from?"

She hesitated. "I wasn't alone."

Breena rested her hands on Meikah's shoulders. "I know you think you're helping, but you're not. Not really. This isn't the way to deal with it."

"I've spoken to other necromancers. There is no other way." Meikah stepped away from Breena.

"Kellan? He's a necromancer?"

Panic rushed through Meikah. Somehow she managed not to let it escape. Or let her magic get out of control. "While I was in the Arcton Mountains. I spoke to necromancers there." It was technically true.

"Meikah." The word was a shocked whisper. "You never said. You never told us anything about your journey there. What happened? Did they hurt you?" Again she gripped Meikah's shoulders.

"This is why I didn't tell you." Meikah twisted out of Breena's grip. "Why can't you trust me? Why can't you believe that I know what I'm doing?"

"We do trust you," Breena protested. "Why can't

you trust we know what's best? We understand this town. Understand the people in it."

She stared at Breena for a moment before turning away, her shoulders slumping. There was nothing she could say to make her understand. The thread of desperation she'd heard in Breena's voice told her everything she needed to know. Her mother had less of an idea than her about what to do.

"Meikah." Breena stepped around so she could face her. "Please. Stop causing trouble and let the rumours die down. If you don't give people a chance to-"

Meikah interrupted. "To do what? Run me out of town with pitchforks and lit pitch torches? To kill me?" Feeling the magic rise, her hands tightened into fists. She obviously needed to spend more time practising how to control her magic.

Breena shook her head. "No. For them to forget."

"Don't you understand?" Meikah demanded. "They will never forget. Not unless they have something more spectacular to overwhelm that memory."

"I don't want anything to happen to you." Breena again reached for Meikah. "Neither does your father. Can't you see we're both worried?"

This time Meikah sidestepped. "It's too late. Nothing can ever change the fact I'm a necromancer." When Breena gasped, her gaze fixed on Meikah's hand, she looked down to see lightning crackling around her fist, the silhouette of a dragon visible on the back of her hand. Shock raced through her, the magic vanishing. She slowly raised her head to look at Breena.

Breena opened and closed her mouth, retreating step by step until her back collided with the wall.

Weariness washed over Meikah. "See. Even you're scared of me. What makes you think those who barely know me will react any better?"

"It's not fear. It's surprise. Your hand…" Breena's voice trailed off and she remained pressed against the wall.

Meikah started to argue. Instead, she shook her head. "I need some sleep if you expect me to attend the Dark Blade Academy today." She strode to the bed, slipping off the soft soled boots as she drew back the covers. "Not that attending the academy is of any use to me. It's not going to help me learn how to control my magic."

Breena came away from the wall slightly. "Where did you get those clothes?"

There was absolutely no way she could come up with a plausible answer. She was too tired to think clearly. "I'm going to sleep." She dropped onto the bed, turning her back on Breena. Closing her eyes, she listened to the silence. She remained still, ignoring the temptation to turn and see what Breena was doing.

"We're not scared of you, Meikah. And we do trust you. You have a lot to learn that we'd rather you didn't learn the hard way." The sound of the door opening and closing punctuated the words.

Meikah rolled over to find she was alone in her room. She stared at the flickering light of the candle, eventually getting up and putting it out before returning to bed. The faint light of the coming day crept in around the edges of the curtain. It felt like she'd barely fallen asleep when a banging on the door woke her. Groaning, she struggled out of bed, about to open the door. She looked down at the clothes she wore. She didn't need anyone else in her family asking where they'd come from. "What?"

"Grandfather Harlen's here and wants to talk to you," Ena called through the door.

Meikah groaned again. She eyed the window, wondering if she should slip out of it and head to the academy. "Can't you tell him I'm not here?" She changed her clothes as she spoke. Clothes more suitable for attending the Dark Blade Academy.

"It wouldn't help. He'd just come up here and check for himself," Ena said through the door.

Meikah's stomach grumbled. She needed something to eat, but didn't feel like facing Harlen. That would be enough to ruin anyone's appetite. She bundled up the outfit she'd worn early that morning. "Tell him I wasn't here." She opened the door and grinned at her sister.

"I am not about to lie for you."

Her grin didn't dim. "No need." Striding across the room, she slipped out the window, taking the Assassins Of The Dead outfit with her.

"Meikah." Ena hung out the window. "Are you trying to kill yourself?"

Meikah laughed. "If I have to listen to a lecture from Grandfather Harlen, someone will probably die. And it won't be me." She dropped to the ground below, running away from the house, ignoring Ena who called out after her. Her smile faded along with her laughter. She couldn't help thinking about the dragon silhouette that had formed on her hand. Maybe the words she'd jokingly spoken to her sister weren't that far from the truth. She needed to practice more. A lot more.

Reaching Fable, she found the front door was locked. Peering through the glass of the window, she could see no one in the shop area. She hurried around the back and, finding that door unlocked, slipped inside. It was empty. Taking several steps forward, she closed the door. Where was everyone? Had something happened? "Amiel?" Surely the necromancer spirit would be here. And Rafe should be downstairs asleep in the basement, but she didn't want to disturb him. No one came. "Amiel?"

Amiel strode into the kitchen from the hallway. "Do you think I'm some dog to come at your bidding?"

"Sorry. Where is everyone?"

Amiel strode out of the kitchen without answering.

She hurried after him. "I'm sorry. I was worried about everyone. The shop isn't open." She followed him down the stone stairs to the basement. The trapdoor had been left open.

"And you think that gives you permission to holler for me?"

"How else was I meant to find you?" She stopped at the bottom of the stairs. A bewitched flame lantern hung from the ceiling casting a soft glow over the area. "Where is everyone, Amiel?"

"Mace is asleep. Do you think I care where the rest of them are?" Amiel demanded. "We don't need others here with their demands and getting in the way."

Livia prowled down the stairs, her gaze on Amiel. "Do you ever do anything other than complain? I could hear you in the kitchen the moment we came inside." She turned to Meikah. "You hungry? Shade is making something to eat before we have a sleep." Livia made a face. "Or should I say take turns at having a sleep." She faced Amiel again, not waiting for Meikah's answer. "Get up there and watch the shop. Let us know if someone comes in."

Grumbling and complaining, Amiel went upstairs.

Chapter Nine

Meikah stared at the empty stairs. She hadn't expected Amiel to give into Livia's demands. "How do you get him to do what you ask?"

Livia chuckled. "Threats. And being willing to follow through on those threats."

"Oh." Meikah followed Livia up the stairs. "Aren't you worried he'll retaliate?"

"He can't. Or at least he can't hurt us. It's part of the deal he made with Danton. He can only retaliate so far." Livia grinned as she entered the kitchen. "And I made no promise not to hurt him."

Shade was cooking bacon and eggs. "Are you tormenting Amiel again?"

Instead of answering him, Livia laughed before turning to Meikah. "Hungry?"

Meikah nodded, her stomach rumbling at the smell of food. "I snuck out of the house this morning so I didn't get a chance to eat." She glanced at the clothes she held. "What should I do with these?"

"Leave them in the bathroom. Someone will collect and wash them." Livia grinned. "Someone other than me."

Meikah hurried outside, leaving the outfit in the bathroom before returning inside where Shade was serving up the first lot of food, putting on more for himself. They sat at the table and Meikah explained her comment about sneaking out of the house, following it up with questions about the task Danton had set them.

Livia swallowed her mouthful. "The Duke currently has so many people watching him that it's a wonder he can find enough privacy to use the bathroom. They aren't his people either. Oh, he has his people watching him, but the ones I'm talking about are not the ones he set to keep guard."

"Who are they?" Meikah asked.

Shade joined them at the table, shrugging. "Danton took over from us about an hour ago. He said he'd watch for a bit. Before we could leave, some of those watching the Duke were replaced by others. We couldn't follow all of them. They headed off in different directions."

"Where did the ones you followed go?" Meikah placed her cutlery on the empty plate.

"The Sleeping Giant." Livia sent a look at Shade. "I wanted to go in and see what they were up to."

"It was too dangerous." Shade continued to eat his food.

Meikah stared at Livia for a moment. "The Sleeping Giant."

Livia nodded.

"That's where we found Tobin."

Livia turned to Shade. "See. I told you we should have gone inside."

"It wasn't safe," Shade said.

Amiel stepped into the kitchen. "Someone has entered the shop. They look like they can't afford a single book. Do you want me to chase them out?"

Livia rose to her feet. "No." She glanced over her shoulder as she strode towards Amiel. "We have to return to the tavern."

"Not without help." Shade gathered the empty plates as Livia stepped out of sight.

Meikah rose to her feet. "I'd best go to the Dark Blade Academy."

Shade smiled fleetingly. "Turning up on time won't help get you thrown out."

She laughed. "I suppose not." She glanced at the

hallway entrance. "I might practice for a bit in the basement." It wasn't like she would be noisy and wake Rafe who slept down there in his coffin. She started for the hallway, pausing at the entrance to look back at Shade. "What did Amiel mean about not needing others here?"

"Danton was talking to him about bringing in more Assassins to help. That was after we all left. He mentioned it when he met up with us earlier." Shade continued to tidy the kitchen.

"Oh." Were things that bad? Had something happened after they'd left? She started to ask Shade, but assumed he would have mentioned if it had. She headed down the stairs to the basement. Maybe she should forget about turning up to the academy and focus on training. Reaching the bottom of the stairs, she drew her dagger, staring at it as she tried to bring lightning to the blade. Nothing happened. She could go upstairs and collect the weapons made of night steel, but she really wanted to learn how to control her magic when it came to ordinary weapons. What if she accidentally made lightning dance across her blade while she was at the academy?

She narrowed her eyes as she stared at the blade. Why couldn't she do this? With the way the trainer looked at her, that Danton had organised, and the way the tone of his voice had slowly changed as he'd taught her, there must be something she was doing wrong.

"Whatever you're doing, it's obviously not working."

Meikah turned to see Amiel on the stairs behind her. "Do you think I don't know that?"

"Then try something different. The sooner the idiot that's trying to teach you doesn't have to turn up here in the afternoon, the better." Amiel strode down the stairs, stepping past her when she got out of the way.

"How? I don't do magic. So how can I try something different when I don't know what my options are?"

"Clearly you don't do magic," Amiel said dryly.

She wanted to argue his comment. It was a little hard to argue something that was true. "I've spent my life as a templar. I've had no need of magic."

"Then I guess you better figure it out before you end up killing someone. Like the one who's training you."

Anger raced through her and for a moment she didn't blame Livia for using threats to keep Amiel in line. Especially with the smile he gave her. Then it struck her, like a bolt of lightning. "Or someone I'm working with, like Mace."

Amiel stalked towards her. "You will stay away from him." He pointed a finger at her.

"I don't want to kill anyone. Not the one training me, not Mace and not any of the others I work with. Why do you think I've been training every afternoon?" Meikah demanded.

Amiel glared at her a moment longer. "If I train you, then you stay away from Mace."

"That isn't up to me. Danton usually tells us who we're to work with. And to truly stay away from him, I'd have to stop coming here. I'm not about to do that." It was one of the few places where she felt at home these days. Where she could be herself and not hide who she was.

"You get him killed, or harm him, and I will make you pay," Amiel warned. "And don't bother telling me necromancers can't die. You try losing your body and you'll see it's as bad as death."

"Then teach me so I don't accidentally hurt him." She studied his expression trying to figure out what he was thinking. Or even if he was likely to agree. She was about to ask him if he was still willing, considering she wasn't going to stay away from Mace, when he spoke.

"Tell the idiotic sorcerer his services are no longer required. You'll be here every afternoon. And you will not complain about the methods I use to teach you."

Chapter Ten

The tone of Amiel's voice caused a shiver to run through Meikah. What had she got herself into? An image of her lightning striking the bandit, in draconic form, came to mind. She had very little choice. The one currently teaching her wasn't helping. "All right. But I don't know how to contact the sorcerer."

"Do I have to do everything? I'll see that he's notified," Amiel snapped.

"Thank you."

Amiel glanced at the dagger she continued to hold. "Stop trying to fill that with your magic. It's not the weapon you're filling. You need to extend your power from your body so it encases it." He strode up the stairs.

She stared after him, questions filling her mind. They would have to wait until the afternoon. Her gaze was drawn back to the dagger and she thought of what he said. She felt power stir within herself and did as he suggested. Lightning flared up around the dagger. She grinned. Amiel had taught her more in a few minutes than the trainer had been able to teach her in days. What would he be able to teach her in an entire afternoon? She forced the lightning away before she sheathed the dagger. It was probably past time she headed to the academy.

Arriving at the Dark Blade Academy, Meikah hurried along the empty corridors to the room her class was held in. When she stepped inside the classroom everyone fell silent as they turned to face her. She wanted to turn around and head straight back outside. She held herself still, meeting the gaze of the trainer as she tried to ignore the eight students who stared at her, daggers drawn due to the moves they'd been practising.

The trainer's eyes narrowed. "What makes you think you are so special you can turn up when you wish?"

She started to lower her gaze out of habit. No one deliberately annoyed a trainer. Holding her ground, when she would have preferred to retreat, she forced herself to continue meeting the gaze of the trainer. She needed to get herself thrown out of the academy.

Apologising and being meek wouldn't do that. "I attended Lady Eris' dance last night. I didn't get home till late. I considered sleeping till noon, but thought I should probably put in an appearance before then." She strolled inside. At the trainer's expression, laughter nearly escaped. No wonder Kellan tended to play pranks on everyone and go out of his way to annoy some of them. This was actually a little more fun than she thought it would be. She'd never seen that stunned expression before. One mixed with anger, shock, disbelief and something else she couldn't define.

"Is this your way of saying you slept in?" the trainer demanded.

Meikah eyed the distance between her and the trainer. The many emotions in the trainer's expression had vanished, leaving only anger behind. "You make it sound like it was an accident."

"Are you saying you deliberately slept in when you were meant to be here, training." The trainer spoke the words slowly and carefully as if to someone who had only begun to learn the language.

Meikah smiled. "That's it. Exactly. I deliberately slept in. I could have done with a few more hours sleep though." She yawned, covering her mouth as she did so.

Silence filled the room. No one moved and no one spoke.

Meikah wanted to check what the rest of the students were doing as the silence lengthened. But she refused to show fear. She kept her gaze on the trainer. Surely the trainer wouldn't harm a student. Or at least not deliberately.

The trainer's gaze swept the room. "Everyone continue to practice the moves I showed you." The trainer's lips twisted into a smile. "I will show Meikah what she has missed so far of the lesson."

Meikah stared at the two daggers the trainer drew. Maybe this hadn't been such a good idea after all. She'd expected the trainer to throw her out of the class.

"Take out your daggers and get over here," the trainer ordered.

Drawing her dagger, having only worn one with her sword, she strode towards the front of the room keeping her head up and shoulders straight. She wasn't about to let the trainer know how concerned she was. Although concern didn't begin to encompass the mixture of emotions that rushed through her. Right now, she would have preferred to face a dozen zombies.

"Where is your second dagger?" the trainer demanded.

Meikah eyed the trainer's weapons. Maybe two dozen zombies would be easier. "I prefer a sword to a dagger." Meikah forced herself to shrug, trying to keep her tone light and unconcerned. "But I've kind of grown accustomed to a sword and dagger combination." She dreaded to think what her parents would say when she returned home this afternoon. Considering she felt a little horrified at the words she spoke, her parents were probably going to be extremely shocked. She shied away from thoughts of Harlen. Her grandfather would be livid.

The trainer nodded to the sword that hung at Meikah's side. "Even using the sword with your dagger, you couldn't match what I can do with two daggers."

Meikah laughed. "I should hope not considering how long you've been training compared to me." She barely managed not to wince at the words she spoke. She was going to be in so much trouble. Harlen would be waiting for her when she arrived home.

"Are you refusing to train?"

Meikah shook her head. "No. Just pointing out that your greater experience means you should do better than me."

"Then let us see exactly what you are capable of." The trainer attacked without warning.

Meikah barely managed to block as she drew her sword. The flurry of attacks drove her back and all she could do was block each one. Although she was surprised she managed to block the attacks. The fights against spirits and zombies had obviously helped. A dagger nearly got past her defences and she twisted out of the way, blocking the second dagger.

"Why are you in the basic class?" The trainer didn't stop attacking. If anything, she picked up her pace.

Meikah had no idea what to tell her. It took her a moment to come up with something. "Probably because I don't use two daggers."

"Then this isn't the place you belong." The trainer didn't slow her attacks.

Meikah wanted to tell the trainer she wasn't saying anything she didn't already know, but was kept too busy trying not to let either dagger slip past her defences.

"Why did you bother to turn up if you're not interested in being here?"

And there was another question she couldn't answer. Not only because she was too busy trying to defend herself. Would they refuse to throw her out if she told them that was what she wanted? There was no way she'd be able to quit. None of her family would allow that. Not her parents and not her paternal grandparents. Isha would stand by her no matter what choice she made. So would Maksim.

The trainer stopped abruptly, her gaze sweeping the room. "Did I tell the rest of you that you could stop and watch? We are not the entertainment. You want to be entertained, visit the theatre. Now keep practising."

Meikah barely managed not to grin as the students began to practice again. At least they'd given her a few minutes break as the trainer walked amongst them, snapping out comments on their form. She listened, taking note of all the information. Most of it wouldn't apply to her, but some would be useful considering she used one dagger. When the trainer returned to her, she wanted to groan. Why couldn't she practice with a student? The trainer could hassle one of them for a change. She tried to remind herself that she'd forced this response, but it didn't help. Not when all this was because of how people had reacted to learning she was a necromancer.

Anger rushed through Meikah and she felt her magic stir. Fear rushed in, blending with the anger, making the magic want to escape. She focused on blocking the trainer's attacks, trying to ignore her magic, pushing the anger and fear from her. This was the last place she could let her magic escape.

Keeping her emotions even didn't help. She tried to figure out what was different, but was kept too busy blocking the attacks. Then it struck her. The trainer was making her work harder and she barely managed to block. She wasn't in any danger, but her magic obviously thought differently. And no matter what she told herself, she couldn't override the instinct to fight with everything she had. Relief rushed through her when the trainer stopped again, stepping back. The magic started to subside, close to the surface if she needed it, but no longer about to escape.

"Can I help you?" the trainer demanded, her gaze focused on a point past Meikah.

She turned to see who the trainer was looking at.

Kellan grinned at Meikah, a picnic basket in one hand, Mace behind him. "Not at all." He strode into the room. He stopped in front of Meikah. "Ready to come on a picnic with us?"

The trainer came forward, shifting Meikah to the side, her gaze remaining on Kellan. "Leave. Now."

Mace strolled in to stand beside Kellan. "We don't plan to stay. We came to collect Meikah." He turned to Meikah. "You ready to go?"

The trainer spoke before Meikah could. "I am teaching a class here. She certainly is not ready to go."

Chapter Eleven

Meikah was past ready to go. She sheathed her sword and dagger, turning to Kellan and Mace. "Where are we going?"

"If you walk out of this room I will send a message to your family," the trainer warned.

"No need for that," Kellan said. "I'm only inviting Meikah. Not them."

"It won't be to invite them to a picnic," the trainer said.

"That's good then," Kellan said. "I didn't bring enough food for extras."

Meikah managed not to laugh at his comment, although some of the students giggled. From the glare the trainer sent them, she wasn't impressed. "I'm ready to go." Or at least get out of here before things went crazy. Her magic was too close to the surface.

"I did not give you permission to leave," the trainer said.

Meikah started to tell the trainer that she didn't need permission.

Kellan interrupted. "How about if the three of us beat your eight students then Meikah can go without a problem."

The trainer looked from Kellan to her students and back again. "You think the three of you can take on eight Dark Blade Academy students and win."

Kellan inclined his head. "As long as we can fight with whichever weapons we prefer. After all, aren't they meant to be able to fight against any weapon?"

Meikah started to protest. How were the three of them meant to take on eight students, even ones in a basic class? Especially with her magic so close to the surface.

"Accepted." The trainer turned her glare on the students. "If you fail, each one of you will remain back this afternoon for extra training."

Meikah wanted to demand what Kellan had been thinking. With an incentive like that, the students were going to be trying their best to win. And her magic would know that. Yet she couldn't protest. How had the situation become so complicated? Her gaze was drawn to Kellan as he set the picnic basket against the wall. She tried not to sigh. Of course things were complicated. Kellan was involved.

Kellan drew a sword and dagger, facing the students. "Rules?"

"Lose both your weapons, and you're out," the trainer said. "Someone draws blood on you, then you're also out."

Mace drew a dagger, fire pooling in his left hand. He moved to stand at Meikah's side, Kellan standing on the other side of him.

One of the students lowered their daggers. "He's a sorcerer. That isn't fair."

"Are you saying you're giving up before the fight has begun?" the trainer demanded.

The student took half a step back, raising his daggers. "No."

The trainer sheathed her daggers, clapping her hands together a single time, the sound loud in the silent room. "Begin."

Meikah attacked immediately, before the student in front of her was ready since both daggers went flying. Her magic became easier to push down, a smile forming as she turned away from the student that had been so easily disarmed. The smile faded as she fought the next student, who was more prepared.

Her magic didn't stir, this one was no threat either.

She heard weapons clatter to the floor, but didn't have time to check. A second student joined the first, both focusing on her. And from their expressions, they were determined to make her pay for the unexpected fight and the threat of remaining back to train this afternoon. Meikah's smile returned. They weren't as difficult to face as a horde of zombies, or the trainer.

One of the students behind Meikah yelped, the sound followed by another weapon hitting the floor. "He made my dagger hot. That has to be against the rules."

Mace chuckled. "You think a sorcerer is going to go easy on you? I barely heated the metal. You could have held on if you'd wanted to."

"No excuses," the trainer snapped.

A third student, who'd been helping another fight Kellan, joined the attack on Meikah and she was forced to only block, unable to attack the three of them. Her magic rose and she fought against it as she struggled to watch all three students. One attempted to circle around behind her. She tried to convince herself that she wasn't in any danger, but the way the students attacked made her think otherwise. Her hand grew warm and she glanced at it, relieved to see the silhouette of the dragon hadn't formed. She needed to end the fight before she accidentally hurt someone.

Retreating, she angled so she could see the three of them.

"Running away, are you?" one of the students asked.

Kellan joined Meikah, having taken out the student he'd fought. "None of you could be that lucky." He attacked the closest student.

Meikah went after the other two, determined to defeat them before she lost control of her magic. Within seconds, their daggers were lying on the floor, a line of blood forming along the wrist of one of the students. A triumphant feeling raced through her and she stumbled when Kellan bumped roughly into her. She started to berate him for his action, stopping when she realised the magic was easing and had been about to escape before Kellan had bumped her.

Kellan grinned, giving Meikah a single nod, his opponent disarmed and glaring at him. He turned to the trainer. "Maybe you should have joined in and given them a hand." Sheathing his weapons, he strode to the side of the room and collected the picnic basket. "Thanks for the exercise." He looked from Meikah to Mace. "You two ready?"

Mace sheathed his dagger. "I'm starving."

Meikah tried to ignore the grim silence, broken

only by the occasional student muttering under their breath. She couldn't hear what they said, but had a good idea. None of it would be complimentary. Turning away from their daggered looks, Meikah followed Kellan and Mace from the room.

Kellan draped an arm around Meikah's shoulders. "Do you think we should have warned them that we've had more training than them?"

"They didn't stand a chance," Mace said. "I bet not a single one of them has ever had any life or death fights."

Meikah glanced at the picnic basket as they stepped outside, her mood lightening at their comments. "Is that the only reason you collected me?" She wanted to ask if there was a message from Danton, but this wasn't the place.

"We want to have something to eat before we go to bed and thought you might like to join us. Were you expecting a different reason?" Kellan asked.

"Who's keeping watch?" Meikah asked.

"We'll tell you everything later," Kellan said.

They fell silent, striding through the town, not speaking until they stopped at an immaculate park that ran past the front of half a dozen mansions. Mace took the blanket from the basket and spread it out on the neatly trimmed grass. Meikah studied her surroundings. This was the kind of neighbourhood her parents would love to live in. One not far from the castle. She sat on the blanket, taking the plate of food Kellan handed her.

Mace stretched out along one edge of the blanket. "I think I want sleep more than I want food."

"I can always eat your share if you want." Kellen held a plate out to Mace.

Mace leaned up on one elbow, taking the plate. "You couldn't have let me sleep for another hour?"

Kellan filled his own plate with food. "At least you got some sleep."

Mace looked at Meikah. "What did you do to upset my great-grandfather?"

"Uhmm." Meikah glanced away.

Mace sat up. "That good?"

"Now I want to know," Kellan said.

Meikah looked from one to the other, doubting she'd get away with not answering. Her gaze came to a rest on Mace. "I might have threatened your life."

Kellan chuckled. "That'd do it. Did you go into graphic detail?"

"It wasn't like that. It's about me accidentally killing someone because of my lack of training. I pointed out that it might be Mace." She looked at Mace. "I wouldn't deliberately hurt you."

Kellan lowered his voice. "And there's our prey, coming out of the mansion across from us."

Chapter Twelve

Her mouth full of food, Meikah couldn't ask Kellan what was going on. She frowned when she saw Tobin head towards the street.

Kellan took the plate from her. "Invite him over."

Meikah finally swallowed her mouthful. "I don't think he likes me very much after he found out I'm friends with a vampire."

"Trust me," Kellan said. "Invite him over and be friendly towards him, but don't deny your friendship with Rafe." Kellan grinned. "I've got a plan."

She groaned. "Like the last one?"

"Have you heard the rumours flying around?" Kellan set her plate to the side. "They're getting better with each telling. Now go and invite him over before he gets too far away."

She got to her feet with a wistful look at the food. Striding towards Tobin, she sighed. She should know by now that Kellan couldn't be talked out of any of his plans. "Tobin." She raised a hand to help catch his attention, hurrying forward.

Tobin stopped, turning in her direction. His questioning expression changed to one of disinterest.

Remembering Kellan's vague instructions, she smiled at Tobin. "I thought you were staying at Lord Barnet's."

Tobin looked past Meikah to where Mace and Kellan remained on the blanket. "What do they think of you being friends with a vampire?"

Her smile faded. "You don't like vampires?"

"To them, we're food."

She wanted to argue his comment, but could think of no polite way to do so. "Speaking of food, are you hungry? We're having a picnic and I thought you might like to join us since you probably don't know a lot of people being new to town."

"I have plenty of friends in this town. Ones that understand the realities of life." With a sharp nod, Tobin continued along the street.

Meikah stared after him for a moment before she returned to Kellan and Mace. "That didn't go very well. I hope that wasn't the only plan you've got because I'm pretty sure that whatever it was, it's not going to work."

"Tell me what happened," Kellan said.

Meikah eyed the plate that was out of reach. "Can't I eat first?"

Kellan handed over the plate. "Try and wait until you've told us everything."

She quickly went over the conversation before returning to the food. The smile Kellan gave her, as she spoke, had her worrying about what he was planning next. She wasn't sure if she should ask.

"Now we have to figure out where he'll be tonight for the next part of the plan," Kellan said.

Meikah glanced at the mansion across from them. "This is why we had a picnic? So Tobin could look at me like I was some bug he found under a rock. I thought his response meant you'd have to come up with a new plan."

Kellan grinned. "The plan is working perfectly. Until he found out you like vampires he was interested enough to follow you from the ballroom last night."

"No, I think he was more interested in finding out how well I know the Duke." Meikah had some more of the food from her plate.

"It doesn't matter why he's interested, as long as he is," Kellan said.

Mace was once again stretched out along the edge

of the blanket. "Does that mean we can go back to Fable and I can return to bed now?"

"As soon as we've finished eating." Kellan put his and Mace's empty plates in the basket while Meikah continued to eat, packing away the rest of the items he'd taken out to serve the food.

Meikah swallowed her mouthful. "I want to know what the rest of the plan is."

"We'll wait until Rafe is awake so I don't have to explain it twice." Kellan took the empty plate she handed him and put it in the basket.

Meikah pointed a finger at Kellan. "As long as you explain it and not give us a handful of information and surprise us with the rest at the last minute."

Mace chuckled as he rose to his feet, taking the picnic basket. "According to Kellan, that's the best part."

Meikah got out of the way so Kellan could pick up the blanket and shake it. "Maybe for him. Not for everyone else."

After he put the blanket in the basket Mace held, Kellan draped an arm around Meikah and Mace's shoulders. "Give it time. You'll grow to love it." He grinned at her. "As much as you love me."

She elbowed him in the ribs as they walked along the street. "I doubt it."

"You're right. How could you love anything as much as you love me?" Kellan asked.

She slowly shook her head. Before she could reply, she realised they weren't heading in the direction of Fable. "Where are we going now?"

"To accidentally run into the Duke. I have a letter to deliver to him," Kellan said. "I hear he's dining at the Duke's Rest today."

"I'll see the two of you back at Fable." Mace slipped out from under Kellan's arm. "Don't wake me when you get in." Grinning, he headed off in the direction of Fable, taking the picnic basket with him.

"Isn't the Duke being watched?"

Kellan nodded. "Which is why you're going to take exception to something I say and do something that will make me stumble into the Duke."

"Do you ever get bored with making plans?" She had no idea how she was supposed to make him stumble.

"Never." He grinned. "The more complicated, the better."

She sighed. "Why do I think your plan for this evening falls in that group?"

"It's a brilliant plan. Even Danton agrees."

"He does?"

"Must have. Otherwise, he would have said more than 'don't get caught'."

That didn't reassure her at all. If anything, it had her more worried about what he planned. "I've got a feeling I'm due for a lecture when I get home this afternoon. I probably won't have the chance to help with any plan."

"Then you don't go home. Wait until after Tobin has become your new best friend."

She drew away from him so she could see him better. "My new best friend. Are you serious? How is that possible?"

"You'll see, but right now, we have a letter to deliver." Kellan nodded at the carriage pulling up in front of the Duke's Rest.

A shiver ran through her. She had a bad feeling the encounter with the Duke wasn't going to be as easy as Kellan had said. When was anything involving Kellan simple?

The Duke and Duchess were helped from the carriage, guards surrounding them. Kellan strode towards them, the Duke waving him through when guards stopped him from approaching. He tugged Meikah along with him.

"Your Grace, I'm surprised to see you here." Kellen

stopped in front of the Duke, giving the Duchess a nod. "Your Grace."

The Duchess glanced at the Duke's Rest. "Should we be concerned about your plans for the day, Kellan?"

He laughed, tugging Meikah closer. "I've been warned that if I'm not on my best behaviour after last night, someone will never forgive me." He smiled at Meikah.

She tried to ignore the fear that raced through her. How did she always end up in these situations? She pulled away from Kellan, glaring at him. "Can you blame me?"

Kellan faced her, trying to capture her hand again. "Meikah–"

"No. I'm not about to let you charm me." She pushed his hand away from her.

He stumbled backwards, running into the Duke. Turning to face him, he patted his jacket. "Sorry, Your Grace. Didn't mean to run into you. Let me straighten your jacket for you." He tugged on the garment.

"That won't be necessary," the Duke said.

"There you go. All done." Kellan stepped back with a grin.

"I think you better see about straightening out

other problems." The Duchess' gaze rested momentarily on Meikah before returning to Kellan.

He laughed. "You're probably right, Your Grace. As always." He gave a shallow bow to each of them. "Enjoy your meal." He glanced at Meikah. "I'll see what I can do about straightening out my own problems."

Chapter Thirteen

Meikah barely managed to bow to the Duke and Duchess before Kellan grabbed hold of her hand and tugged her along the road. She drew her hand out of his grip. "Will you stop doing that?"

"I thought you wanted a sleep. I know I want one," Kellan said.

Walking beside him, she looked him up and down, seeing the weariness not only in his face, but also in the way he walked. "I forgot you haven't slept yet."

He grinned at her. "Does that mean I get to hold your hand again?"

Her lips reluctantly curved into a smile and she slowly shook her head. "I'm surprised you don't end up in more trouble than you do."

Laughing, Kellan draped an arm around her shoulders. "So am I."

They fell silent, only the sound of their feet on

the cobblestones making any noise. Arriving at Fable, they found Livia serving a customer, giving her a nod as they headed through the curtained doorway and upstairs.

Amiel was coming down the stairs. He glared at Meikah. "Getting Mace on your side won't help you."

Meikah frowned. "I don't understand what you're talking about."

"Telling him about our deal," Amiel said.

"I wasn't trying to get him on my side. I was explaining why you're going to train me." She was too tired to get into an argument with Amiel. "We can start once I've had a sleep." Slipping past him, she headed to her room. It wasn't until she'd set aside her weapons and had stripped down to her undergarments, that it struck her. She stood beside the bed, staring down at it. She couldn't think of this as her room. Thoughts tumbled through her mind, but she didn't come to any decision. She was torn. It would be better to move in here, less problems, but she didn't want to leave her family. Not yet. She wasn't ready.

Forcing the mess of thoughts from her mind, she lay down, pulling the covers up, surprised she was able to fall asleep so quickly when the thoughts kept returning. She was woken by Amiel standing over her. For a moment she worried about what he'd do with the way he glared at her.

"Did you expect me to wait all afternoon for you? Weren't you the one who demanded I train you?"

She kept the covers pulled up. "I'll meet you in the basement."

He glared at her a moment longer before he strode away.

She remained where she was, wondering if she was crazy to have forced him to train her. Throwing back the covers, she got out of bed and dressed. No, this was the best option. Maybe another necromancer would be able to teach her. The sorcerer didn't seem to be helping. She started to take her night blades, changing her mind at the last second. Causing lightning to crawl along them was easy in comparison to normal metals. It was no point taking the easy path. That wasn't going to help her learn.

An hour later, when Amiel again berated her for her lack of progress, she stared at the sword she held, wondering why she'd chosen it over the night blade. Anger flared and with it her magic, lightning crackling along the blade. For a moment she stared open-mouthed at it, surprised at the power. When she realised lacey dragons played amongst the lightning she dropped the weapon. The lightning vanished.

"Now what is your problem?" Amiel demanded.

"There were dragons. Amongst the lightning." Her gaze remained fixed on the blade of her sword lying on the stone floor of the basement. "Lightning dragons."

"If you're going to be distracted by every little thing, you're going to get yourself killed," Amiel stated. "And others along with you."

"It wasn't a little thing." She finally managed to drag her gaze away from the blade to look at Amiel. "They were dragons. How am I meant to make my magic work properly when it's not normal?"

"You think anything about magic is normal?" Amiel demanded.

Meikah shrugged. "I don't know anything about magic. Other than what I've been taught the past few days."

Amiel pointed a finger at her. "That is why you should stay away from everyone. If anyone should be chased out of town to live in the Arcton Mountains, it's you."

She took a step back, his words more painful than she wished. "No one deserves being chased out of town. At least not for no reason."

"Risking those around you is a reason," Amiel said. "What about your family? You seem to care about them. What if you kill one of your family?"

"I'm not about to kill anyone." She spoke the words with a clenched jaw, matching Amiel's glare. "Not my family and not Mace."

"That's good to know."

Meikah turned to see Mace coming down the stairs.

"What are you doing down here?" Amiel demanded.

"Letting Meikah know food is ready and it's almost dark. We need to plan tonight's entertainment." Mace stopped halfway down the stairs.

Meikah wasn't certain if she should head upstairs for food or remain and finish the argument with Amiel. Picking up her sword, she sheathed it. "I have no plans to get anybody killed. My magic isn't that uncontrollable." She was certain she was getting better at this. Hadn't she managed to fight the students today without her magic escaping? "You can teach me tomorrow afternoon." She walked towards the stairs, glancing over her shoulder. "Actually teach me, not just complain about what I can't do."

Mace led the way to the kitchen. "Danton is back. He needs us to go to the theatre tonight before we do anything else. To give the Duke a chance to pass along any messages he might have in reply to the letter Kellan gave him earlier today."

Meikah sat at the table, glancing around at everyone who was seated with her. Livia was arguing with Danton about needing to stay behind to keep an eye on the bookshop while he slept. Shade pointed out that she'd gone to the Arcton Mountains while he'd remained behind. Kellan offered to let her attend the theatre instead of him, earning a glare for his offer. Meikah smiled as she listened to them.

Mace put a platter of roast vegetables and sliced beef in the middle of the table, handing around plates and cutlery. "Help yourselves." He sat at the table with them, turning towards Livia. "Did you want me to stay here so you can go to the theatre with Kellan and Meikah?"

"Why does everyone think I want to go to the theatre?" Livia demanded. "I want to be in on the stuff that's happening later."

"Do you think I should remain at the bookshop all the time so you can join in on the more interesting things?" Shade asked.

"No, no one needs to stay here. We don't always have someone staying at the bookshop." Livia helped herself to the food on the platters.

"Someone needs to be here in case of an emergency," Danton said. "Between my brother being watched and SAV hunting down vampires, we don't know what might happen."

"I could stay here if Livia wants to go the theatre," Meikah offered. She quickly added when Livia glared at her, "And do whatever needs doing afterwards."

"We need you for the plan to work," Danton said. "For whatever reason, Tobin showed an interest in you. It doesn't matter if it's because he thinks you have the ear of my brother or if it's for a different reason. We can use it to our advantage."

"I don't want to go to the theatre," Livia muttered.

Kellan chuckled. "I don't know, I think you're starting to protest a little too much. Maybe trying to hide a secret desire to attend?"

Mace laughed at the glare Livia sent Kellan. "You might want to consider sleeping with one eye open, Misty."

Meikah smiled at the nickname Mace used for Kellan.

"Who has time to sleep when they're having all the fun?" Kellan asked breezily.

Livia pointed at him with her knife. "You might consider taking Mace's advice."

Rafe entered the kitchen. "Did anyone find out where Tobin will be this evening?"

Danton shook his head. "That will be yours and Mace's task." He looked from one to the other. "You're to stay together. Or at least within sight of each other. Just because they call themselves the Society Against Vampires doesn't mean they aren't willing to kill others who get in their way."

Chapter Fourteen

Meikah stopped with a forkful of food partway to her mouth. "I have nothing to wear to the theatre."

"I arranged for several dresses to be made for you," Kellan said. "Another arrived while you were downstairs training with Amiel. It's on your bed."

"You can't… It's not right… You didn't…" Her voice trailed off.

"You'll need them for some of the work we do," Danton said.

"Oh." Meikah had no idea what to say. She wanted to ask who had paid for them, but couldn't bring herself to voice the question. Not when she wasn't sure how she'd feel about the possible answers.

Kellan grinned. "The dress from me is still to come. The one you'll wear on our evening out together."

She started to protest.

Amiel entered the kitchen. "Someone is knocking on the shop door. Isn't anyone going to answer?"

Danton rose to his feet, motioning for everyone else to remain seated. "I'll see who it is. Eat while you have the chance. Most of you will be kept busy this evening."

"Except for Livia," Kellan said.

Livia glared at him.

Meikah turned to Kellan when Danton left the room. "What is the plan for this evening?"

"I drink your blood," Rafe said.

Meikah stared up at him, not sure she'd heard correctly. "You do what?"

Rafe crossed the space between them in a blur of movement. He raised her hand off the table. "You need to appear to struggle and we'll make sure that Tobin comes along to save you. You need a reason to doubt vampires."

"What if he attacks you?" Meikah asked. "Or the rest of his group come after you?"

"No one will know who the vampire is that attacks you," Kellan said. "We want you to tell him that you'd never have expected vampires to behave like that because of your friendship with Rafe."

"I wouldn't want you harmed by them." She continued to allow Rafe to hold her hand, meeting his dark eyes. She caught a flicker of fire in them. "I don't like the idea of you and Shade following Tobin this evening. That sounds too dangerous. For you more than Shade."

"Have you forgotten I can turn into a bat?" Rafe asked.

"No. But bats can be caught," Meikah said.

Shade put his cutlery on his empty plate, rising. "Are you ready to go?"

Rafe held Meikah's hand a moment longer before he let her go, turning to Shade. "Yes, but I need to have my dinner first."

"Remember it can't be anyone unwilling," Kellan said.

"There's a tavern that caters to vampires." Rafe headed towards the hallway.

Livia rose from her seat. "Wait up, Rafe." She waited until he faced her before she continued speaking. "Maybe you shouldn't go to places like that while SAV are in town." She held out a hand, wrist up. "You can have mine if you want."

"Thanks for the offer, but there's no need to put you through that pain." With a nod and a smile for Livia, Rafe stepped into the hallway.

Meikah looked at Livia. "How bad does it hurt?"

Kellan spoke before Livia could. "He won't be

feeding from your wrist. Vampires prefer to feed at the neck. It wouldn't be logical for a vampire who is supposedly feeding from you against your will to feed from your wrist."

"Oh." Meikah wasn't sure how she felt about that.

"It won't hurt," Kellan said. "The only problem you'll have will be remembering to struggle."

She wasn't sure she wanted to know why it'd be difficult to struggle. Before she could decide, Danton entered the kitchen.

"I received a report of another two vampires missing." Danton sat heavily on the seat he'd been using earlier. "That's three. That we know about." He turned to Kellan. "This doesn't change anything. Don't take any risks in an effort to try and sort it out sooner."

Grinning, Kellan rose from the table. "I better get ready for the theatre." He looked from Meikah to Mace. "So should you two."

Meikah hurried after Kellan as he headed up the stairs. "Do you think the vampires are dead?"

Kellan shrugged. "I'd like to think they're somehow alive, but I don't have much hope that they are."

"How do we know they haven't killed more

vampires than the three we've been told about?" Meikah stopped by her door.

"We don't. We need to find proof as quickly as we can so something can be done about them. If they've befriended nobles, we need strong proof so those who would stand up for them can't argue the facts." Kellan entered his room.

Meikah remained in the hallway a moment longer, Mace having already entered his room. No wonder Danton had told Kellan that nothing had changed. Even she was tempted to do something reckless if it meant finding the proof they needed. How many innocent vampires would die before something could be done about the Society Against Vampires?

Inside her room, she found another evening gown with matching slippers. This one was bronze. She slowly shook her head when she saw the thigh sheath and dagger were also with the gown. Someone had obviously collected it. Probably Kellan.

It didn't take long to dress and she came out of the room to find Kellan waited at the end of the hallway for her. He smiled. "That bronze coloured material suits you as well as the burgundy does." He held out a hand. "The carriage is out the front waiting for us. So is Mace."

She placed her hand in his and walked down the

stairs with him. She waited until they stepped outside before she spoke, keeping her voice low. "Are you planning to do something reckless?"

"Would you mention it to Danton if I was?" Kellan faced her as the two of them came to a stop out the front of the shop, glancing at the coachman.

"As long as SAV is here, Rafe's life is in danger."

Kellan gave a single nod at her words, momentarily tightening his grip on her hand. "Exactly." He continued to the carriage, handing her in.

No one spoke on the trip to the theatre, conscious of the coachman driving the carriage. There was also no chance to speak when they arrived at the theatre where they were ushered to their seats. Meikah sat on one of the comfortable seats in the private box that belonged to Kellan's family. The balcony was on an angle to give her a good view of the Duke and Duchess who sat in the central private box, their balcony lavishly decorated. Her gaze was momentarily drawn to the seats below, where her family typically sat when they went to the theatre.

Kellan leaned close. "Look at Lord Barnet's private box across from us. It's probably the first time it's been used in years."

Meikah looked directly across to see Tobin sat in one of the seats of a private box, a middle-aged man beside him. "We need to find a way to let Rafe and Shade know."

"They'll figure it out soon enough," Mace said. "Servants tend to talk."

Chapter Fifteen

Meikah glanced around the theatre, recognising some of the faces. She nearly fell off her seat when she saw Harlen and Sirena were in the audience. She felt like sinking below the lip of the private box so neither of her grandparents could see her. What would she say to them if they came over to talk to her at the end of the play? She glanced towards the stage, wanting the play to begin. She didn't want them coming over before the play started either.

"Is there a problem?" Kellan asked.

Meikah again glanced at her grandparents. "No, only a lecture I'm trying to avoid."

Kellan chuckled. "I don't think they'll cause a scene here."

The lights dimmed in the theatre and Meikah realised they were bewitched flames. When silence fell over the theatre, the lights around the stage brightened and the curtain rose. She focused on the stage, enthralled as the play began, far better than the last one she'd seen. She was so caught up in the story, she forgot all about her grandparents until the curtains fell and everyone rose to their feet to applaud. She looked for her grandparents, unable to see them. Were they headed up here?

Kellan took her arm. "Time to visit the Duke."

Meikah looked across the way to the crowded private box. "I doubt you'll get close enough to see him."

"He'll manage somehow." Mace led the way.

When they reached the Duke and Duchess' private box, Meikah watched as Kellan made his way closer to them. When he wasn't far from the Duke, he stumbled, bumping into him. Glaring at someone in the crowd, he said, "No need to push and shove." He turned, fixing up the Duke's garment. "Sorry about that."

"Seems to be becoming a habit, Kellan," the Duke said dryly.

"I'll try not to do it again," Kellan said.

"Meikah."

She turned at the sound of her name, surprised it was Tobin.

"Will you introduce me?" Tobin nodded towards

the Duke, Kellan remaining near him and talking to both the Duke and Duchess.

She pretended to misunderstand him, not wanting to introduce him to the Duke. Who knew what he planned to do if he got close. "You've already met Kellan and Mace was at the picnic earlier today. Don't you remember?" She almost smiled when his jaw tightened.

"You misunderstand–"

Kellan joined them, interrupting. "Tobin, isn't it?"

Tobin glanced past Kellan at the retreating Duke and Duchess. "Yes, if you will excuse me." He started to move away.

"Why don't you join us?" Kellan asked. "The Duke mentioned he's attending Lady Eris' supper this evening and invited me along."

Tobin faced Kellan. "Supper, you say."

Kellan nodded. "I'm sure it can't be easy being new to a town. My carriage should be out the front waiting for us." He grinned. "The coachman is a marvel at finding a park at busy locations such as the theatre. I have no idea how he manages." He slung an arm around Tobin's shoulders. "Plenty of space for one more."

Meikah followed behind Kellan and Tobin, having caught a glimpse of Tobin's expression before he'd masked it and Kellan had ushered him towards the exit. If Kellan hadn't mentioned the Duke, she was certain Tobin would have pulled away from him.

Mace walked beside her, leaning in close to whisper in her ear. "Try and avoid introducing him until after you've convinced him to become friends."

"I don't want to introduce him at all." She couldn't imagine anything good would come of letting him get close to the Duke.

"I don't like the idea of him getting close to the Duke either, but you might need to at some stage. We don't want to make him suspicious."

Meikah was unable to answer as they'd reached the carriage. Like Kellan had said, it was waiting out the front for them. Before she entered, she caught a glimpse of Shade who disappeared into the crowd once he'd met her gaze. She sat beside Kellan who talked to Tobin, sitting across from him. She was glad Kellan kept up the small talk on the way to Lady Eris' mansion. She had no idea what to say to Tobin. All she wanted to do was demand how he and his father could be a member of the Society Against Vampires.

Kellan gestured for Tobin to exit first then helped her out. When Kellan and Mace didn't immediately follow, she turned to see what they were doing.

Kellan had his back to her. When he hopped out of the carriage, Mace remained inside.

"Hope you don't mind if I have an early night," Mace said.

Kellan waved him off. "Of course not. I'll see you in the morning." He slung an arm around Meikah's shoulders, doing the same to Tobin. Behind them, the carriage rolled away. "After we say hello to Lady Eris we'll see what's on the menu. She has an amazing cook."

Meikah wished she could ask what was going on, but she couldn't exactly do that when Tobin was on the other side of Kellan. The moment Tobin pulled away from Kellan and hurried ahead to greet Lady Eris, she took the opportunity to ask, moving closer so she could whisper in Kellan's ear. "Why did Mace leave?"

"To deliver the Duke's letter to Danton." Smiling, Kellan let go of her and stepped forward to greet Lady Eris.

Meikah joined him, following him to the tables laden with food once that was done. The supper consisted of a buffet and people served themselves, wandering around talking to each other as they picked at the food on their plates. It seemed to be more of a social event than gathering where you concentrated on eating. Meikah scanned the crowded rooms as they wandered through them, Kellan nodding and occasionally stopping to speak to people. Like at the theatre, she recognised some of the faces, but it didn't appear that her grandparents were here. That didn't surprise her since they weren't friends of Lady Eris, but there had always been a chance that one of their friends might have invited them along. It was a relief she wouldn't have to worry about them until later. Although she dreaded to think what Harlen would have to say. It wasn't going to be pleasant.

Tobin rejoined them, having wandered off to talk to someone else at one stage. "How well do you know the Duke?"

Kellan handed his plate to a servant, draping his arm around Meikah's shoulders. "The Duke seems very fond of Meikah. Or at least he doesn't berate her when we get in trouble. Only me."

"Maybe because he knows you're the one who gets us into trouble to start with," Meikah said.

"Did you see where he went?" Tobin asked.

Meikah shrugged. "It's so crowded in here."

Kellan draped an arm around Tobin's shoulders. "If you do see him, let Meikah know. Or the Duchess.

She was saying that she wants to find out what the Duchess thought about the scarf she gave her."

Meikah managed not to laugh at the expression that fleetingly crossed Tobin's face when Kellan draped his arm across his shoulders. "Actually, I think I see…" She let her voice trail off, handing her almost empty plate to Tobin. "Oh, I do." She slipped through the crowd before either of them could follow her.

Chapter Sixteen

Taking a deep breath, Meikah tried to remain calm. It wasn't that she was worried, it was more that she was excited about trapping Tobin with their plan. Whatever the Society Against Vampires planned to do, they weren't going to get away with it. Dreyton was her town, not theirs. She slipped inside an empty room, leaving the door open. It was a sitting room, a fire crackling in the fireplace with several armchairs positioned around it.

Rafe entered the room by the window. He was wearing dark clothes and a mask that covered the top half of his face, a dark cloth tied over his hair. "Shade will let us know when Tobin is coming close."

"What if Tobin doesn't find me?" Meikah asked. "What if I was too quick for him to see which direction I took?"

"He seemed pretty determined to follow after you.

And annoyed at Kellan for slowing him down." Rafe laughed softly. "More annoyed when Kellan put his arm across his shoulders."

"I noticed he was annoyed by that," Meikah said.

Rafe took her hand, drawing her to the armchairs. "We might as well get comfortable while we wait. I wanted to ask earlier if you were all right after training with Amiel. Don't take anything he says personally."

"I won't." She remained standing. "At least he's helping me figure out how to use my magic." Her gaze was momentarily drawn to their hands. "You never told me what Sarette said. When we were leaving Longview. You weren't hoping I'd forget, were you?"

Rafe continued to hold her hand, smiling down at her. "Not with how persistent you are." He stepped close, running a finger along the side of her neck. "It bothers you, doesn't it. My need to feed on blood."

"Not exactly bothers me." She looked into his dark eyes. "How can you have any respect for someone who is little more than a meal?"

"It is more than being a meal, Meikah." He lowered his head, his lips against her neck. "Shade warned me Tobin is coming this way."

It took a few seconds for his words to sink in,

then his teeth did. There was a sharp, fleeting pain, followed by a warmth that washed over her, making her relax in his arms. She clung to him, her head tilting back further.

Rafe pulled away slightly. "Fight me, Meikah. You're meant to be fighting me." He lowered his head again, his lips pressed against her throat. This time he didn't feed from her.

She struggled against the inclination to continue clinging to him. "Let me go." She raised her voice a little. Enough that someone walking past would hear, but not those further away. She tried to push him away, twisting and turning in his embrace, his arms tightening around her, his lips remaining pressed against her neck.

Tobin burst into the room, drawing a stake from beneath his jacket, running towards Rafe.

Meikah started to get between Tobin and Rafe, automatically wanting to protect him. Rafe pushed her aside and she stumbled. By the time she'd gained her balance, Rafe was out the window and she was alone with Tobin.

"What happened?" Tobin demanded. "Was that your friend from last night?"

Meikah shook her head, touching her fingers to her neck. Drawing them away, she saw blood on them.

"I don't know who it was." Remembering she was meant to be playing the victim, she added, "I was so scared. He was much stronger than me. I didn't realise how strong they are. Rafe has never seemed that strong."

Tobin held a linen handkerchief out to her.

Taking it, she dabbed it against her neck. "Rafe would never have done something like that to me. He's my friend. I thought vampires were different from what the stories make them out to be. He's the only vampire I've ever known." She managed to shudder in what she hoped wasn't too exaggerated a manner.

"You can't trust any vampires. We're only food to them."

She stepped closer to Tobin, the handkerchief bunched in her hand. "He said he'd return. That I couldn't stop him from visiting me whenever he wanted." Another step and she had to look up at Tobin. "What can I do?"

"I know people who can help. People who can protect you. Even from your so called friend." Tobin put his stake away.

"But Rafe would never hurt me." She paused a moment. "At least I don't think he would."

"It's all an act. They lure you in before going for

the kill. Some like the hunt, others like to betray. But it's basically all the same. You can't trust a vampire."

She wanted to argue his words. Lowering her gaze, she fought against the urge. "How do I know I can trust your friends?" She looked up at him again. "I barely know you."

"Why don't I introduce you to some of them tomorrow? They're meeting at a tavern around midday."

Meikah lowered her gaze again to hide the humour she guessed was probably visible in her eyes. The Dark Blade Academy wasn't going to be impressed. That was if they hadn't already thrown her out. "I'd like that."

"Shall I collect you from your home about half past eleven tomorrow morning?"

She frantically tried to think of another option. Heron wouldn't let her go anywhere if she turned up at home during the middle of the day and he was at home. He'd probably march her back to the academy. She looked up at Tobin again. "I promised Kellan I'd join him for the midday meal. Can I bring him along with me? I'd hate to break a promise. We could eat at the tavern first."

"Like you said, I don't know him well enough to trust him," Tobin said.

"When I tell him-" She broke off to dab at her neck with the handkerchief. She slowly shook her head. "It all seems like a bad dream."

"They have to be stopped." He gripped her shoulder. "Don't you understand? It's them against us. The dead should remain dead."

The fanatical look in his eyes caused a shiver to run through her. It brought back the chant the Society Against Vampires members had been saying in the street when they'd returned from the Arcton Mountains. The rest of the words were burned into her brain. "I felt like some beast raised for the slaughter, bred only to provide sustenance for someone else."

"We're not cattle for them to feed on."

His words echoed the ones that had been spoken that night by the Society Against Vampires members. If she'd ever had any doubts, they were well and truly put to rest. Why would someone use their chants if they weren't a member of their faction? "How will I sleep knowing he's out there?" She dabbed her neck again with the handkerchief, mentally apologising to Rafe who would have remained nearby. She'd make sure he knew she hadn't meant a single word she'd spoken.

"I can teach you how to use a stake so next time

one tries to feed, you can use it against them." His grip on her shoulder tightened.

She wanted to pull away, not just from his grip, but also the look in his eyes. It was clear he wouldn't stop until all vampires were dead. She thought of the dagger in the thigh sheath. No, his death wouldn't help. They needed to know who gave the orders. Who chose which vampires would be hunted and killed. "Can you? I'd feel so much better knowing I had some way of defending myself. I can use a sword and a dagger, but against a vampire, they seem useless."

"They are. A stake through the heart and then removing the head is the best way to be certain the vampire will never come back to life. Some burn the bodies, but I find leaving them behind for vampires to discover can help rid a town of the cowardly ones."

She latched onto his words, hope for the missing vampires rising. As far as she knew, no dead vampires had been found. "Doesn't that mean they'll go somewhere else? Wouldn't it be better to do something more permanent?" When he examined her face, not speaking for a moment, she had to fight the urge to back away from him.

He smiled. "You'd think. But fear of what is coming can be a powerful tool in a fight. There are those that hunt vampires, ones that all vampires fear. The vampires that leave carry with them the fear of what is coming to other towns."

She wanted to demand if he was talking about the Society Against Vampires, but she couldn't exactly do that when she was pretending to have no idea about what was really going on. "How do you know all of this?" She nearly winced at the look of suspicion that crossed his face. "I feel so unknowledgeable in comparison. I really thought vampires could be trusted as much as the next person."

"That is what they'd have you believe. We're only cattle to them. A necessary food source that is considerate enough to take care of themselves. Do you want me to collect you tomorrow?"

"I was meant to meet Kellan at the Duke's Rest at midday."

His grip tightened on her shoulder again. "Do you like being a meal?"

"Of course not."

Kellan entered the room. "What happened? I didn't expect you to be gone so long."

Tobin let go of Meikah, stepping back. "I'll call for you at eleven thirty." He began to stride from the room.

Chapter Seventeen

Meikah hurried after Tobin. "Wait."

Tobin glanced at Kellan. "The answer to your earlier question is no." He started to leave again.

She grabbed hold of his arm. "I'll meet you out the front of the Dark Blade Academy. I won't be at home tomorrow." She let go of his arm when he glanced at her hand, barely managing not to point out that he'd been the one grabbing hold of her earlier.

Inclining his head, Tobin strode from the room.

Meikah stared after him.

Kellan moved to her side. "Rafe said you were having problems convincing him."

"Not exactly. The problem is more that he didn't want you to come along too." She faced Kellan. "I have no idea where he wants to take me or what his plans are. And he won't let you come with us."

Kellan captured both her hands, the handkerchief

still bunched in them. "Do you think we'd allow you to go in alone? We'll keep watch over you. You might not see us, but we'll be there keeping you safe."

Rafe entered the room through the window. "I won't be. I can't help you during the day."

Meikah drew her hands from Kellan's grip, her gaze momentarily resting on Rafe's lips. "That's probably why they meet during the day."

Kellan slung an arm around Meikah's shoulders. "The rest of us will keep an eye on you until Rafe can join us."

His words didn't reassure her. There were so many things that could go wrong. "Can we leave now? I'm tired."

Shade came in the window. "Tobin left a few minutes ago." He looked at Rafe. "Do you want to follow him with me?"

Rafe nodded. He turned to Meikah and Kellan. "I'll see you tomorrow evening."

He was out the window before Meikah could say anything. Not that she knew what to say, other than to apologise for the words she'd said to convince Tobin to introduce her to the Society Against Vampires.

Kellan took the handkerchief from her, slipping it into his pocket before he took her hand. "I'll take you back to Fable so you can get changed before I walk you home."

"Then you'll be on the streets alone."

"Mace will be at Fable. He can walk with us." He stopped by a door that led outside. "You might want to avoid people." He glanced at her neck. "Rafe made sure Tobin couldn't miss seeing that he'd fed on you."

She raised her hand to her neck.

Kellan captured her hand before she could make contact. "Dried blood. No damage. Only two small holes and a lot of dried blood. Without all the blood, the holes would probably not have been noticed."

Nodding, she pulled away from him and hurried outside. She remained close to the mansion, not wanting to stray too far from it while she was alone. Out the front, she spotted Kellan's carriage and was seated inside by the time he joined her. "I thought we weren't meant to go anywhere alone."

"There are some rumours we don't want to start." He took hold of her hand. "How do you feel after having a vampire feed on you?"

She shrugged. Telling him she felt unsettled didn't feel right. That was something she should tell Rafe before she told him.

"It's odd the first time. Especially when it's your neck."

Startled, she tried to see his expression in the shadowy interior of the carriage. "Who fed on your neck?"

Kellan chuckled. "I never kiss and tell." He lowered his head so he could speak softly near her ear. "In case that's what's worrying you."

She shifted across on the seat. "Kellan-"

He interrupted her. "Please don't say anything. At least leave me with my false hopes."

At the teasing note in his tone, her lips reluctantly curved into a smile that she immediately tried to stop, knowing he could see in the dark. "Have you considered you shouldn't have any hopes? Not even false ones?"

"Shouldn't I?"

She looked away at the serious note in his voice. Once again, she had no idea what to say. Relieved that they'd arrived at Fable, she hurried inside. About to head upstairs and get changed, she heard voices in the kitchen. Entering, she found Danton, Mace and Amiel talking. Or arguing, in Amiel's case.

Kellan entered the kitchen. "What happened?"

Danton held up a scrap of paper with a rusty coloured streak on it. "I intercepted this."

Kellan took the paper from Danton, reading it

aloud. "A pity he isn't more like his cousin. He wouldn't allow vampires in the town."

"It isn't a threat," Amiel said.

Danton faced Amiel. "I doubt they're going to come straight out and threaten him on a piece of paper that could fall into the wrong hands. Or the right hands according to your view."

Kellan examined the piece of paper. "Do I take it from this stain that the one delivering it didn't survive?"

"He's alive. Injured, but alive." Danton nodded towards the hallway. "In the basement. No one goes down there without a mask. And keep the trapdoor shut. He remains our prisoner until we have enough evidence to take down the entire organisation. Then he'll be my brother's problem."

"Rafe sleeps down there," Meikah protested.

"The prisoner is chained, gagged and blindfolded. I doubt he'll escape, but just in case we'll chain Rafe's coffin for him and Amiel can keep an eye on our prisoner," Danton said. "How did the two of you fare?"

Kellan gave a brief account of the evening. When he'd finished, Amiel turned to Meikah. "Is this your way of getting out of training tomorrow afternoon?"

Danton spoke before she could. "No one can train

in the basement while we're keeping a prisoner there. He might accidentally come to harm."

"Rather him than Mace," Amiel said.

"No training in the basement," Danton said firmly.

Amiel made a wide, sweeping gesture. "Then we'll train in here."

When Danton nodded, Meikah said, "Wouldn't that put more people at risk?" She didn't want to harm any of the Assassins Of The Dead.

"They'll get out of the way if they have any sense." Amiel faced Meikah. "I'll see you here in the afternoon." He started to walk away.

"In the morning, before I go to the academy." Meikah had no idea if there'd be time to train after she'd been to the meeting with Tobin.

Amiel paused at the entrance to the hallway, glancing over his shoulder to nod at her. He continued walking. "I'll see what information I can get out of the prisoner."

"Don't kill him," Danton called after Amiel.

"Once we've changed out of these clothes do you want to help me walk Meikah home?" Kellan asked Mace.

Mace nodded.

Meikah was almost at the hallway entrance when

she remembered the letter Mace had delivered. She turned to face them. "What did the Duke say?"

"He's lost four of his spies in the past week and one of his personal guards. He seems to be constantly shadowed and has suffered several unusual accidents. He's considering sending the Duchess to the capital to visit her brother," Danton said.

"Her brother?" Meikah asked.

Danton took the intercepted note back from Kellan. "It seems his daughter has been spending time with the King's son."

"I wonder what that might mean for the Duke if they marry," Kellan said.

Not interested in listening to the gossip, Meikah left them to it while she went upstairs and changed. She laid the dress and dagger on the bed, not sure what to do with them. Stepping out of the room, she found Kellan in the hallway waiting for her, dressed in normal clothes. She gestured to her room. "My dress-"

"Leave it there, I'll see that it's laundered." Kellan touched his fingers to his own neck. "You might want to finish cleaning up before you go home."

Chapter Eighteen

In the bathroom, Meikah looked into the small mirror that hung on the wall above a narrow table scattered with various objects belonging to those who lived above Fable. She lightly touched her fingers to the small marks on her neck, looking worse than they were from the amount of blood smeared across her skin. Turning the tap on, she leaned over the cast-iron tub, scooping water in her hand to wash away the blood. She couldn't help think of the many people in Dreyton who didn't have access to running water. Mostly only the nobility had gravity fed bathrooms and occasionally kitchens.

Once she was certain her neck was clean, she turned off the tap and had another look in the mirror. The two small holes were barely noticeable. She ran her fingers over them. The memory of Rafe feeding returned. Would she have fought off a vampire? She hadn't realised what it would be like. Surely if it had been a stranger she would have fought. Yet she couldn't help wondering if the feeling that had washed over her would have made her remain in their arms, a willing meal.

Pushing unsettling thoughts aside, Meikah strode inside, joining Kellan and Mace who led the way out the front door of the shop. The night was quiet, giving her too much time to think. She focused on her surroundings instead. The road was empty and the shops and houses they passed were silent and dark. Reaching her home, she stared at the lights that seemed to be on in every window of the house. It didn't bode well. She had a bad feeling her grandfather was probably waiting for her. She really didn't want to face a lecture.

"Are you going in the front door or your window?" Kellan asked.

She glanced at Mace when he chuckled. "I want to say window, but I have a feeling that won't help."

"Want me to check if someone is in there waiting for you?" Mace asked.

She shook her head, straightening her shoulders. "I better get the lecture over and done with."

"Did you want us to wait here in case you need us to walk you back to Fable?" Kellan asked.

She was extremely tempted to say yes. "No. I'll see you in the morning when I train with Amiel. Before I train with him, not during. I'd rather not hurt anyone." She smiled wryly. Which was always a possibility with how Amiel annoyed her.

Kellan drew her back to him when she started to walk away. He kept an arm around her waist. "Sometimes it takes leaving to learn how you fit into a place."

"I'm not running away." And she wasn't about to let them chase her off either.

"It's not running. It's finding a strategic location." With a grin, Kellan let her go and stepped back.

She stared up at him for a moment, wishing there was more light so she could see his expression clearer. Maybe she should have Amiel teach her that first. Especially with how often they spent in the shadows. "Goodnight." She looked at Mace, giving him a single nod before she turned and strode towards the front door. It was locked. Sighing, she knocked, listening to the approaching footsteps. A glance over her shoulder showed Kellan and Mace were out of sight. She had no idea if it meant they'd left the area.

The door swung open. Heron remained in the way, glaring down at her, the lamplight clearly showing how angry he was.

Meikah had to force herself to hold her ground, raising her chin to meet her father's gaze. "Are you going to let me inside." When he didn't answer immediately, she feared the answer might be no.

Heron stepped back, letting her inside before closing the door. "Where have you been?"

"Is that Meikah?"

She almost closed her eyes at hearing Harlen's voice. He stepped into sight a few seconds later, followed by Sirena. She was tempted to go back outside at the sight of both her grandparents.

"What have you to say for yourself?" Harlen demanded. "All anyone could talk about at the theatre was you and Kellan. Has he proposed to you?"

"No." At least he'd given her one question she could answer. It wasn't like she could say anything in her defence.

"You need to find better quality friends," Sirena said. "His family might be from the nobility, but even they regularly distance themselves from him and his antics."

"I had other friends, but they disappeared when the rumours of me being a necromancer started," Meikah said.

"They aren't exactly rumours now, are they?" Harlen demanded.

Yet something else she couldn't argue. "Are people talking about me being a necromancer?"

"You know very well they aren't," Harlen snapped.

"That's not the point," Heron said. "You're still causing the gossips to talk."

She pressed her lips tightly together, trying to contain the words that wanted to escape.

"You cannot expect to get away with the same behaviour that some of the children of the nobility manage to get away with," Sirena said. "People will tolerate more from them than they will from the lower classes. Even from those of the middle class."

"The Dark Blade Academy expects an end to your carryings on. You will attend every lesson and you will stop causing rumours," Harlen ordered. "They'll give you one more chance. After that, you're out."

"It's not like they really want me there. Not the students and not some of the trainers." Meikah glared at Harlen. "None of you listened to what I wanted either."

"You aren't welcome at the Templar Academy," Heron said.

She started to argue his words, shaking her head instead. "I'm going to bed." She started for the stairs.

Heron grabbed hold of her right wrist, tugging her away from them.

She struggled against his grip, anger and magic flaring. Dragon shaped lightning streaked out from her hand, knocking Heron back. He landed on the floor, causing shocked gasps from his parents.

Sirena ran to his side. "Are you hurt?" She tugged him into a sitting position, checking him over.

Heron brushed her hands away, struggling to his feet.

Harlen loomed over Meikah. "You would attack your father? Who do you plan to attack next? Me? Your grandmother? Or maybe your mother and sister."

She looked from Harlen to Heron, speechless. She didn't want to hurt her family. Backing away, she shook her head. "No."

"I saw you. Do you think you can deny what we saw?" Harlen demanded.

She continued to shake her head, the anger swamped by fear. "I have to-" She had no idea what she needed to do.

"None of us will tolerate this kind of behaviour," Harlen stated.

Meikah's gaze was drawn to her father, who looked dazed. She wanted to ask if he was unharmed. The words didn't come. She couldn't stay here. Not with Harlen berating her and Sirena asking Heron if he was fine. He still hadn't replied. "I have to go." Spinning, she yanked the front door open, running outside. Behind her, she heard her father call out for her to return, the first words he'd spoken since being knocked to the floor. She didn't stop, racing to the corner of the street.

"Meikah." Kellan stepped in front of her, his arms going around her as she crashed into him. "What happened?"

"They'll come after me." She pulled out of his grip, running down the main road.

"Who will come after you?" Mace kept pace with her, along with Kellan.

"My father. My grandparents." She again pictured her magic knocking her father to the floor. It brought to mind the bandit she'd done something similar to. At least she hadn't knocked Heron unconscious.

"What happened?" Kellan asked again.

Chapter Nineteen

Meikah glanced at Kellan as they ran under a lit lamppost. "Why were you out the front? I thought you would have left by now." The last thing she wanted to do was tell anyone she'd attacked her father.

"When Heron didn't let you inside straight away, we stayed to see what would happen," Kellan said.

"We were going to sneak in your window and see if you were all right," Mace added.

"Are you all right?" Kellan asked.

She didn't answer immediately, slowing her pace. "I don't know."

"Did someone hurt you?" Kellan demanded.

Again she didn't answer immediately. "I attacked my father." Her words were soft.

"What did he do to you?" Kellan asked.

"It was an accident." She slowed to a walk as Fable

drew near. "He grabbed my arm and I tried to pull away. The lightning dragon attacked him." The scene replayed in her mind. She stopped at the door of Fable and turned to face them. "I need to learn how to control my magic. I can't let it escape whenever I get angry or someone grabs me."

Kellan moved close to her. "You will learn how to control it. Magic takes time to understand and wield. It isn't like you've had anything to do with it before now. Give yourself a chance." He grinned. "Either that or we'll find people who deserve to be attacked and you can hang around them."

Meikah reluctantly smiled. "Like Tobin."

Kellan nodded. "Exactly."

"Are we going inside now?" Mace asked.

Meikah opened the door, relieved to find it wasn't locked. Livia was sprawled across the counter in cat form. Her sleek, black fur gleamed in the lamplight.

When Kellan attempted to pat her, she swiped at his hand. He grinned. "You shouldn't be on the counter."

Livia growled, but remained where she was.

Smiling, Meikah entered the hallway, she looked between the doorway ahead of her and the stairs. She took the stairs, not wanting to discuss attacking her father with anyone else. It had been bad enough telling Kellan and Mace. What was she going to do? She didn't want to leave home. And where had Breena been? Why hadn't she come to the door to see what was going on? Had she waited in her bedroom again?

Having no answers to her questions, she paused outside the door to her room, turning to Kellan who'd followed her up the stairs. "Goodnight."

Kellan's gaze momentarily rested on her lips. "Is that as good as it gets?"

"Goodnight, Kellan." She said the words more firmly, slipping inside the room, surprised to find the candle was lit. Closing the door, she stripped down to her undergarments before dropping onto the bed. What was she going to say to her father next time she saw him? Still trying to figure that out, she fell asleep.

Meikah woke to Amiel standing over her. She wanted to roll over and go back to sleep. Visions of attacking her father kept her from doing so. "I'll be downstairs soon."

Amiel didn't speak, leaving her room without even a nod in acknowledgement.

Rising from the bed, she found a pile of folded clothes had been left on the chest of drawers. Clothes that someone had collected from her bedroom. She was both thankful she didn't need to wear yesterday's clothes and slightly annoyed someone felt they could raid her bedroom. As soon as she was dressed, she headed downstairs to find Kellan and Mace at the table eating their morning meal, a third plate set for her.

"Who collected my clothes?" She sat at the table.

Kellan grinned. "No need to thank me."

She glared at him. He looked far too cheerful for how little sleep they'd had. "I hadn't planned to. Do you think I'm incapable of getting my own gear? I don't need you going through my room looking for things. How would you like it if I went through your bedroom?"

Kellan's grin didn't falter. "Did you want a guided tour? Of my room here and at my parents' home?"

She glared at him, tempted to throw something at him, and possibly at Mace too when he chuckled. Focusing on her food, she tried to push her magic away.

"That's what your problem is," Amiel said.

She looked over her shoulder to see he watched her. "What is my problem?"

"You keep pushing your magic away when you should be embracing it." Amiel lifted her right hand. "I saw the shadow of a dragon for a second. Then it was gone. If you keep pushing it away you'll never be able to understand it. When it becomes too great for you to handle, it will escape with devastating effect."

She tugged her hand from his grip. "What else am I meant to do with it?"

Amiel smiled. "Use it."

"You want me to strike someone with lightning?" Surely she hadn't heard him correctly. Especially since Mace was seated across the table from her.

"How stupid are you?" Amiel demanded. "Using it doesn't mean a lightning bolt. It can be as simple as channelling it into a nearby object. Bewitched flames regularly need to be recharged. They don't last forever."

"I don't know how to make bewitched flames let alone how to recharge them," Meikah said.

Amiel looked skywards, sighing heavily. "A toddler has more skill than you."

Meikah glared at him. Before she could protest, Mace spoke.

"I don't know about that." Mace chuckled. "The stories my mother tells about the disasters I caused when I was a toddler make me think otherwise. At least she's never set anything on fire. More than once."

"That's different." Amiel made a dismissive gesture. "You came into your power earlier than most."

Meikah looked from Mace to Amiel. "That doesn't help me."

"Finish your meal and we'll start with the basics. What made you think you could take shortcuts when it comes to learning magic?" Amiel demanded.

She started to argue, returning to her food instead. Why did everyone keep expecting her to know about magic? She'd been raised a templar.

As soon as the meal was finished, Kellan and Mace made themselves scarce while Meikah remained with Amiel, somehow managing to control her temper even with his cutting remarks and insults about her abilities. She was relieved when she could call a halt, claiming she needed to attend the academy for at least an hour before she met Tobin.

Not that the hour she spent at the academy was any better. Every student she was paired with while they practised, was determined to kill her. Or at least that was the way it felt. The entire time she spent trying to keep her magic under control. When a change of partners was called out, Meikah sheathed her weapons, striding towards the door. She glanced over her shoulder. "I'll see you tomorrow."

"Where do you think you're going?" the trainer demanded.

"I'm meeting a friend for the midday meal." With a smile, she stepped through the doorway.

"Leave the premises and you won't be welcome to return." The trainer followed Meikah as far as the doorway.

Meikah barely hesitated. It was only the thought of what Harlen would say that caused her to hesitate at all. Waving breezily over her shoulder, not bothering to glance behind, she continued along the empty hallway. She had no idea what her family would do about her walking out of the academy, but she wasn't sure she should go home tonight and find out. Giving them time to get over their initial shock might be best.

Chapter Twenty

Reaching the front gates, Meikah looked up and down the road. On the other side, Kellan stepped out of the shadows for a moment, dressed in an outfit to help him blend in, no mask currently on. She smiled at him before he disappeared into the shadows again. Staring at where she'd last seen him, she was surprised to find the area brighten a fraction.

Kellan pulled on his full face mask, nodding at something Mace said.

Shock raced through her, the area dimming. She'd actually managed to do magic. When she'd wanted to. Although she had to admit it had been an accident. Before she could dwell on it any further, she caught sight of Tobin riding towards her, leading a saddled horse. How were Kellan and Mace going to follow her on foot?

Tobin dismounted when he reached her. "I've

brought a nice, quiet mount for you. I wasn't sure how well you can ride."

She took the reins he held out. "Thank you. Where are we going that we'll need horses? I thought we were visiting a tavern in town."

"We aren't going far." Tobin gestured towards the extra horse. "Do you need a hand mounting?"

She shook her head. "No. I'm fine thank you." She forced a smile. "I was looking forward to a walk."

"It's too far to walk," Tobin said.

Meikah nearly glanced in the direction of Kellan and Mace. She managed to stop herself in time. "Can we walk a little bit of the way?"

"Is there something wrong with riding?" Tobin asked.

"No, I was hoping we could walk for a bit. I had some questions to ask you." Again she struggled not to glance in Kellan and Mace's direction.

"What questions?"

She felt like closing her eyes at the suspicion she could hear in his voice. "About vampires. Questions I can't ask Rafe. They're…" She made a vague gesture with her hand as she frantically tried to think of some suitable questions. "Well, they're not the sort of things I'd normally ask him about."

"Like what?" Tobin asked.

"Can a vampire track down humans they've fed on? Is there a way to slow them down? What other weapons can be used against them?" She made another vague gesture with her hand. "There are others, but…" She allowed her voice to trail off.

"Haven't you asked your vampire friend anything?" Tobin asked.

Meikah shrugged. "It seemed impolite." She pretty much knew the answer to the first question and had no need for answers to the second two. Especially not in regards to Rafe.

Tobin took a step closer. "They're hunters. Once they have your scent, they can track you down anywhere. They don't need to have fed on you."

It was the look in his eyes that caused a shudder to run through her, not his words. "Rafe wouldn't hurt me." She made her words sound uncertain. Like it was a question more than a statement.

"After today, you'll know better." He held her gaze a moment longer before he glanced towards the extra horse. "Are you sure you don't need a hand mounting?"

Hearing the finality in his tone, she shook her head. "I can manage." She swung into the saddle, following him as he led the way out of town.

They left it behind, taking the road that went

towards the capital. Regularly checking the area, trying to spot one of her friends, Meikah began to fear she was on her own. All she saw were farmlands, with the forest off in the distance. About to give up searching, she caught a glimpse of a sleek, black mountain cat. Livia was following. She was more than capable of keeping up with a horse. Meikah was surprised at the amount of relief that washed over her. She'd obviously been more worried than she'd thought.

"We're running late." With a glare for Meikah, Tobin urged the horse into a canter.

Meikah did the same, coming alongside Tobin. They left the farmlands behind, entering the forest. Not far in they came upon a small clearing with a dilapidated tavern set back from the road. They slowed the horses, walking the rest of the way. Meikah frowned as she read the faded sign at the front of the tavern. The Dancing Duck? She'd never heard of it before. Although that didn't surprise her since the trip to the Arcton Mountains had been the first time she'd left Dreyton.

Tobin led the way around to the side of the tavern where several horses were tied at hitching posts. He found a spot at the far end, dismounting. "We're the last to arrive."

At the displeased tone of his voice, she kept her distance. She had a dagger and a sword, but from the number of horses at the hitching post, two weapons wouldn't be enough to take on all those who were probably inside. "I thought you said they didn't meet until midday. It's not midday yet."

Tobin checked the pocket watch he drew out, frowning at it before he returned it to his pocket. "Five minutes to. I prefer to be ten minutes early."

Meikah remained silent. There wasn't exactly anything she could say considering she was the one who'd made him late. Deliberately made him late. Following him to the front door, she stepped into the tavern, coming to a complete stop. The place was crowded. There were more people inside than the number of horses had indicated. They'd either walked, were staying in one of the rooms she assumed was upstairs, or there was another place horses were kept.

Tobin glanced over his shoulder. "Are you coming?"

She nodded, following him towards one end of the room, weaving her way through tables and chairs and the people standing around. She remained with a group off to one side when Tobin indicated that was where she should stand. Ignoring the urge to stare at everyone and everything, she glanced around the room, trying not to show too much curiosity about the place. Bodies pressed in around her, many of them towering over her. She also saw a variety of weapons, all of them sheathed or tucked into belts. She caught a glimpse of daggers stuck down the side of the boots of those standing nearby. Her two weapons definitely weren't going to be enough.

A man entered the area in front of her, which was clear of people. He clapped his hands a couple of times, bringing an end to the low hum of conversations. It took Meikah a few seconds to realise it was the middle-aged man who'd sat in the private theatre box next to Tobin. Lord Hemmet.

While he greeted everyone and thanked them for coming, she looked around for Tobin. She couldn't find him anywhere. Lord Hemmet talked about losing his wife and children to vampires and how no one had done anything about it. Nor had he anyone to turn to for help. Now those who had problems with vampires had the Society Against Vampires. Meikah frowned. Why hadn't Tobin mentioned anything about losing his mother and siblings? Surely that would have been the kind of thing you'd mention when trying to convince someone of how evil vampires were.

Around her, those listening made sounds of agreement, some of them shouting out their grievances. She began to worry about what would happen when the crowd became more boisterous as they were slowly doing.

Tobin joined Lord Hemmet, smiling at him when he ended his current tirade. "I assume some of you are uncertain of how little vampires can be trusted."

Meikah was relieved she was looking at him when his gaze fell on her. What would he have thought if she'd been once more scanning the room, taking note of those who were here and cataloguing the entrances to the tavern.

Tobin's gaze swept the room. "Let me tell you, Lord Hemmet doesn't exaggerate in the least. The vampire he speaks of was a trusted family friend. One no one believed would ever harm a single one of the family, let alone kill nearly the entire family. He drained them of blood while they begged him to stop." Again his gaze swept the room.

Meikah wanted to ease her way through the crowd to the edge of it rather than be surrounded by people who muttered agreements. Several called for the final death for all vampires. She kept her expression neutral, all the while holding back the fear she felt for Rafe. She desperately needed to get out of here.

She had no idea how long she'd be able to hide her true feelings. With how much danger she felt like she was in, her biggest worry was that her magic might escape. As it was, she could feel it building. Remembering Amiel's advice, she sent a trickle into the weapons of those standing around her. Not enough to harm, only enough to give a minor shock, as if from static. A grin nearly escaped at successfully putting a trickle of magic into half a dozen weapons. At the last second, she remembered where she was. A smile would have stood out amongst all the angry expressions around her.

A man beside Meikah yelped when his hand rested on the hilt of his sword. He shrugged when his companion asked what had happened. "I don't know. It was like lightning in my sword."

"How strange," his companion said.

Again Meikah struggled not to smile.

Tobin paused in his tirade against vampires to look at the two men. "Do you have a story to share with us?"

One of the men took a step backwards at the glare Tobin directed towards them. He shook his head. "No different to the rest of us. No one cares what vampires do. Or how many they kill. Or the bloodless bodies they leave behind. Or even about those of us left behind to grieve."

Tobin pointed at him. "That is the truth. No one cares except for the Society Against Vampires. All of us here have had those we love stolen from us. And if we don't do something about it, then it will keep happening." A roar of agreement filled the tavern.

Chapter Twenty-One

Meikah wished Kellan could have come with her. She was surrounded by a crowd that could easily turn nasty. And from the way Tobin was encouraging them, that might be what he wanted. "What can we do?" She needed to know what their plans were. "They're stronger than us. How can we do anything against them?"

Tobin's lips curved into a smile, the fanatical light in his eyes increasing. "By attacking together. Alone, we're helpless. As a group, they can't beat us. They can't drain us of blood. They can't kill us. Together we can overpower them."

A roar of agreement again filled the tavern.

Meikah wanted to retreat. She was surrounded by the enemy. She was sure there were bad vampires, but not all of them were the same. Just like not all necromancers were the same. But she couldn't move away from where Tobin had left her. There was no way she could explain that. And she'd already roused Tobin's suspicions enough. Around her she heard the Society Against Vampires' chant. 'The dead should remain dead.'

Tobin joined her, letting another person speak to the crowd, this time a woman who demanded justice for the family she'd lost. "Do you understand now?"

Meikah wanted to put some distance between her and Tobin. "I didn't know you'd lost most of your family to vampires."

"You're not the only one who's been attacked by a vampire." Tobin made a vague gesture towards the rest of the tavern. "You're surrounded by others like you."

She felt terrible about lying to him, but he couldn't attack all vampires because one had killed his family. She placed a hand on his arm. "I'm sorry you had to go through that."

"The Society Against Vampires will make sure no one has to go through the same. They will eventually destroy all vampires. One town at a time."

The fanatical look in his eyes sent a shiver through her. She wanted to tell him that this wasn't the way. That only the guilty should pay, not the innocent. "You said you'd teach me how to use a stake."

Tobin inclined his head. "Later this afternoon. I have a few people to talk to first." He glanced at the crowd around them, the woman now finished her speech and the crowd talking amongst themselves. "While I'm gone, speak to some of those here. Learn their stories. You'll be surprised at the atrocities vampires have committed."

Not knowing what else to do, she nodded. She tried to keep an eye on where he went, but lost track of him over near the stairs leading to the rooms above the tavern. She mingled with the rest of the crowd, slowly making her way across the room so she was closer to the stairs. She reached them in time to see Tobin come out of a trapdoor beneath the stairs. She turned to the woman beside her before Tobin could notice she'd spotted him. "Have you lost family too?"

The woman shook her head. "A good friend."

"I'm sorry to hear that." Once more she had to fight the urge not to say something. It wasn't all vampires who were the problem. She trusted Rafe and she knew there were other vampires who could be trusted. She'd met them in the Arcton Mountains.

Tobin joined her. "Are you ready to leave, Meikah?"

She was more than ready. Past ready. "Yes." She wanted to pull away from him when he slipped an arm around her waist to guide her through the crowded room.

"We'll go out the back. It's closest." He kept his arm around her as they approached an open door not far from the stairs. He let go of her so they could go single file through the narrow doorway.

Meikah hurried ahead so he didn't have the chance to put his arm around her again. Just because she was sorry he'd lost his family to vampires, it didn't mean she trusted him. Out the back, she saw a stable that wasn't in much better condition than the tavern. There were several horses tied up out the front of it and she could see others inside. Amongst the trees behind the stable, she caught a glimpse of Livia. This time the relief that washed over her at learning she continued to have someone she trusted nearby wasn't a surprise. Two against all those who were inside, were impossible odds if Tobin should become suspicious, but it made her feel better to know she wasn't alone.

"Do you have anywhere to be this afternoon?" Tobin led the way to where they'd left the horses.

Meikah couldn't help thinking about the Dark Blade Academy. "I cancelled my plans with Kellan. That was all I had planned for today." Technically, it was true. Attending the Dark Blade Academy hadn't been one of her plans.

Tobin gathered the reins of his horse. "I can teach you how to use a stake if you'd like. There are plenty of barely used rooms at Lord Barnet's place."

"Thank you." Meikah gathered the reins of the horse Tobin had brought for her and swung into the saddle. "I'd appreciate that." Or at least she'd appreciate the chance to spend time with him so she could learn more about the Society Against Vampires. And hopefully gain an introduction to his father. She rode alongside him as they headed back towards Dreyton.

Tobin glanced at her. "Did what you learn at the tavern answer some of your questions?"

She doubted he'd be impressed if she said she hadn't listened the entire time. Part of the time she'd been worried about not letting her magic escape. A wry smile formed. "I was actually a little overwhelmed by everything. By how many people who'd been harmed by vampires. Or lost someone to vampires. It might take a while for everything to sink in." She hoped that covered her if he referred to something she should have heard.

Tobin remained silent for a moment, glancing at her again before he spoke. "Most people don't realise what they're really like. And I'm not only talking about the ones they kill. There are also the humans they keep prisoner to feed on whenever they want. With no care as to how much blood they take each time until eventually, they're bled dry."

The anger in his expression shocked her. She wanted to ask if that had happened to him. Is that why he'd been left alive when most of his family had been killed?

The rest of the journey into Dreyton was silent, Tobin's words hanging over them. Meikah caught a glimpse of Livia a couple of times, but no one else. Tobin didn't even bother speaking to the servant that came forward, to take the horses, when they reached Lord Barnet's mansion.

He didn't speak until they were in the front entrance, alone. "Did you want me to organise something for you to eat?"

She tried to think of a way to decline. She didn't trust him and wasn't about to have any food or drink he offered. "I probably shouldn't eat before practising how to use a stake. It's never good to exercise on a full stomach."

Tobin led her to a drawing room, stopping in a spacious area in the middle of the room. "This isn't the best place to practice, but it's one of the rooms that's rarely used." He drew a stake from out of his boot. It was slim, sharp and made of wood. He pressed it into her hand, wrapping his around hers. "Always carry more than a single stake on you."

She wanted to pull away from him. "I don't own any. Where can I get them?"

"The Society Against Vampires supplies them, but I prefer to carve my own. There's something satisfying about knowing you created the weapon that put the dead to rest." He pressed the point of the stake against his body at an angle. "Push it into the heart from under the rib cage. No need to make the task any more difficult."

Chapter Twenty-Two

She met Tobin's gaze. An unnerving look was mixed with the usual fanatical one. Her hand tightened around the stake. It'd take so little effort to drive it home. She glanced away from him, stepping back and pulling her hand from his grip. "Should we practice with something blunt? I wouldn't want to accidentally hurt you."

Tobin stepped so close that Meikah was forced to look up at him. His lips twisted into a mirthless smile. "Life is never without risk. You can't protect yourself against all harm."

She wanted to protest. Not his words, but the tone he used. Which was crazy. She stared at the stake she held. "How would I stop a vampire taking this from me?"

"Tuck it down the side of your boot."

She did as he ordered.

He grabbed hold of her shoulders. "When a vampire attacks you, don't worry about fighting. They'll expect you to be complacent. Use that to your advantage." He leaned in close, his lips at the side of her neck, his breath warm against her skin. "Practice." He pressed his lips against her neck.

She wanted to pull away from him. She made herself stay in place and reach for the stake down the side of her boot. She pressed it against his body, a little harder than necessary. "Like this?"

He moved back to smile down at her. "Exactly like that." He leaned in close. "Put it away and try again. Make your movements less noticeable."

She did it four more times, each time wanting to argue the need. It felt like he was enjoying it too much. Even the way she pressed the stake against him, harder than necessary, didn't seem to bother him. When she heard a raised voice outside the drawing room, she drew back from Tobin, relieved for a distraction. She recognised Lord Hemmet's voice.

"When I put my journal somewhere I expect to find it exactly where I left it. Not in my room."

"I'm sorry, my lord."

"Don't keep telling me you're sorry. Do as I've

asked. How difficult is it to follow one simple request?" Lord Hemmet demanded.

Meikah wanted to interrupt. His tone and how loud he spoke certainly wasn't a request. She turned to Tobin. "Do you want to see if your father is all right? He sounds upset."

"The servants here have been allowed to do as they please for too many years," Tobin said. "It has led to them becoming insolent and thinking themselves better than those they serve. And they say the Arcton Mountains are uncivilised. At least the servants there know their place. Or they did in the town I visited recently. Now there's an area overrun with vampires. It'll be a pleasure to see something done about it."

Meikah felt her magic rise. The servant hadn't sounded insolent. They'd sounded like they were afraid. She held the stake out to Tobin. "I should probably go home and spend time with my family. They complain I'm never at home."

Tobin didn't take the stake. "Is there another reason you're hurrying off?"

She tried to relax, but it was difficult when Lord Hemmet continued to berate the servant. "All this talk of vampires and learning about the death of you and your father's family has me thinking about how it would feel to lose my own."

He stared at her a moment longer before he took the stake. "Have you any plans for this evening?"

She shrugged. "Kellan often takes me along to whichever event he's been invited to."

"Does the Duke often attend the same events?"

She barely managed not to look past Tobin to where Lord Hemmet continued to raise his voice. How long did he plan to go on? "Sometimes. Shall we let you know what we plan to do in case you'd like to join us?"

Tobin returned the stake to his boot. "I'll escort you home." He turned towards the doorway.

She stepped past him, managing to dredge up a smile. "There's no need. I could do with some time alone. I have a lot to think about. You've shown me so many things I hadn't considered." She stepped through the doorway before Tobin could say anything, stopping behind Lord Hemmet. "My lord, I'm afraid we haven't been introduced."

He spun to face her, glaring at the interruption.

She dredged up another smile. "I'm a friend of Tobin's. Meikah."

Lord Hemmet looked her up and down. Without saying a word, he strode away. The servant scurried off in the opposite direction.

Meikah stared after Lord Hemmet.

Tobin joined her. "He's never got over losing his family."

Meikah faced Tobin. "He still has you."

Tobin's lips twisted into a smile. "Maybe having me isn't enough." He nodded in the direction of the front door. "I'll walk you outside."

She tried not to feel sorry for him as they headed for the front door, but couldn't help it. Surely he was wrong. Lord Hemmet must be relieved that at least one of them had survived. She turned to tell him that as they stepped outside, but his expression was closed and after a single nod, he returned inside. She stared at the timber door for a moment before she strode towards Fable. There was no way she was going home. Not after last night. Or rather, early this morning. It wouldn't be safe for her family.

Before Meikah had walked far, Livia joined her, coming out of the shadows created by shrubs bordering the property of a neighbouring mansion. The shapeshifter grinned. "You should have heard the panic Kellan was in when they realised Tobin had horses."

"He wasn't the only one," Meikah said.

"Lucky you were able to stall him long enough for Kellan to run back to Fable for me," Livia said. "What happened in the tavern? I couldn't get close enough without someone spotting me."

"The place was full. I didn't realise SAV had so many members. I'm pretty sure I saw some nobles amongst them. They remained at the back of the crowd and appeared to be hiding who they were."

Livia slowly shook her head. "Nobles can be idiots. They think a change of clothes will hide who they are. Most don't realise their bearing gives them away." The two of them fell silent, not speaking until they reached Fable, Kellan coming out the front door as they approached. Livia grinned at him. "Did you think I wouldn't manage to look after her?"

"What happened?" Kellan drew Meikah inside, holding tight to her hand.

"It was a meeting." She walked through the shop to the kitchen where Mace, Shade and Danton waited for them. Amiel entered the room moments later. "A really large meeting." She repeated what she'd told Livia before going into further details, at one stage mentioning she hadn't eaten. Mace made food while she continued to speak, serving it before the conversation was done.

"Did you see what was below the trapdoor when it opened?" Mace sat across from Meikah.

"As if she'd be able to see," Shade said.

Mace shrugged. "You never know."

"I was too busy trying to avoid Tobin noticing I'd been looking for him," Meikah said.

"We need to find out what's down there," Shade said. "It might be whoever he takes orders from."

"How are we meant to do that?" Livia demanded. "I couldn't get close. There were too many people about and the place was packed. I could smell all the humans filling the tavern."

"They have to sleep sometime," Mace said.

Amiel glared at Mace. "Why do you always need to throw yourself into dangerous situations?"

"No one will go alone," Danton said. "Two of you can go out there after dark and see what you can learn."

"I'll go since I know where it is," Livia said.

Shade linked his fingers through Livia's. "I'll join you."

Livia smiled at him before she looked at Meikah. "Why did you end up going to Lord Barnet's place?"

Chapter Twenty-Three

Meikah shuddered at the memory of her visit to the mansion. "Tobin wanted to show me how to use a stake." She answered the resulting questions, ending up telling them about Lord Hemmet berating the servant.

Danton stared at Meikah. "We need that journal."

Kellan grinned. "I'll be up for that."

"How are we going to get in there without anyone noticing us?" Meikah asked.

"Tobin wants to meet my brother," Danton said. "We'll see that he does." He looked at Mace. "Find out where my brother will be tonight and I'll arrange an invitation." He turned to Shade. "Go with him. It shouldn't take you long and then you and Livia can see what you can learn about The Dancing Duck."

Livia made a face. "That's such a ridiculous name."

"The original owners bred and sold ducks. They

were told they'd never amount to anything." Danton smiled. "I guess they wanted to make sure no one forgot where they came from in life. My father told me about it during a trip to the capital years ago."

Mace and Shade rose from the table. Mace faced Meikah. "Was that everything? You didn't have anything else to tell us? Like actually stabbing Tobin with the stake?"

Meikah chuckled. "It was close."

Kellan captured her hand, lightly squeezing it before letting go. "I don't blame you. There's something extremely wrong about him."

"If he was kept a prisoner by vampires, he's probably more than a little broken," Danton said. "Be careful how you treat him. I wouldn't want any of you to come to harm."

Livia looked in the direction of the shop. "Someone entered. I dealt with the last customer. It's someone else's turn."

"I'll see to them on our way out." Shade strode towards the hallway, Mace following.

"Don't get caught," Danton called after them.

Finished her food, Meikah rose from the table, not sure what to do next. She was about to ask Amiel if he wanted to help her train when Shade returned to the kitchen.

He remained in the doorway, looking at Meikah. "Your sister is here."

Meikah stared at him. "Ena?"

Shade gave a single nod before he returned to the shop.

Meikah remained where she was. "Ena is here?"

Kellan joined her, draping his arm around her shoulders. "Need me to go with you?"

She wanted to say yes. Pulling away from him, she shook her head, striding towards the shop. She remained behind the counter, her sister on the other side of it. Shade and Mace were nowhere to be seen so she assumed they'd left. "How did you find me?"

"Kellan hangs out here."

Meikah tried to think of something to say. Nothing came to mind.

"They've been looking for you. Our parents. And our grandparents."

Guilt struck Meikah. "Grandmother Isha?"

Ena shook her head. "She keeps telling everyone to stop making a fuss and to leave you alone. That you know where home is."

Relief rushed through Meikah. "I suppose no one is listening to her as usual."

Ena took a step towards the counter. "You have to come home. Everyone is worried."

"Why didn't you tell them where I was?"

"Grandfather Harlen would have come down here yelling."

Meikah grinned. Her sister was probably right. "So you think I should go home and put up with his yelling?"

"You think the rest of us should have to put up with it when you're the one who caused it?" Ena demanded.

Meikah came around the counter. She didn't have time to go home. Rafe was in danger. As well as other innocent vampires. "I'll walk you outside."

"You're not coming, are you?" Ena remained where she was, not shifting even when Meikah took several steps towards the front door.

"Not today." She faced her sister, gesturing towards the door. "I'll come home in a few days. I'll walk you out."

Ena brushed past her. "I can find my own way out."

Meikah tried to ignore how sharp her sister's tone was. How did Kellan manage not to always be in trouble with his family? She followed her sister outside. "What are you going to tell them?"

Ena looked over her shoulder, remaining on the footpath. "It'd serve you right if I told them you don't care what we think or how we feel."

She opened her mouth to argue with her sister. Shaking her head, she closed her mouth instead. An argument wouldn't help. "Tell them lies if you want. I can't stop you."

Ena turned to face her. "What happened to you? You're completely different since you came back."

She let her sister's words sink in. She almost agreed, but deep down, she knew the words weren't true. "No, you're wrong. I'm exactly the same. Maybe you've never stopped to see me properly." The changes were superficial, she was the same person she'd always been.

Ena didn't answer immediately. "I'll tell them I saw you on the road. That you're fine and will come home in a couple of days." She started to move away, turning back again. "Make sure you do. Maybe Grandfather Harlen isn't worried, but our parents are."

Meikah nodded. "I'll see you in a day or two." She watched her sister walk away, turning when she felt someone behind her. It was Kellan. She smiled at him, a barely formed one that was probably filled with the sorrow she felt.

"You can stay here as long as you like."

"I know." She paused a moment. "But I do want to

go home eventually. When I can control my magic better."

He walked inside with her. "You think a day or two will be enough?"

She smiled at him, this one not filled with sorrow. "With the way Amiel has been driving me, I might only need a day."

Amiel stepped out from behind the curtained doorway. "You're not that skilled."

She laughed. "But are you?" When his eyes narrowed, she asked, "Can you teach me some more while we wait to find out what the Duke is doing tonight?"

"Probably the best time to do it. At least Mace isn't close enough for you to harm him." Amiel strode back to the kitchen.

Meikah started to follow.

Kellan captured her hand and drew her back to him. "Don't push yourself too hard. We don't want you harmed either."

She met his gaze. Her breath caught at the look in his eyes. "I…" Her voice trailed off as she tried to capture her thoughts. "Amiel is probably waiting." She hurried away, facing Amiel when she reached the kitchen. He was alone. She was tempted to ask him where Livia and Danton were, but she didn't have the chance. He started snapping out orders.

By the time Mace and Shade returned, Meikah was glad to take a break. Amiel didn't accept excuses and kept her working on each task he set until she managed to get them right. Danton and Livia returned to the kitchen, Kellan following. They sat around the table, Mace grinning at Kellan.

"The Duke is going somewhere I'm not going to like," Kellan said.

"Your parents have a dance this evening," Shade said.

Livia chuckled. "Didn't they tell you not to make another scene at one of their entertainments or they'd be forced to take all your privileges away from you? No allowance, no running up bills at the tailor and no coachman. Your sister will be happy if she doesn't have to share the second carriage and coachman with you."

"Who says I'm going to make a scene?" Kellan asked.

"When do you not?" Livia rolled her eyes. "Drama is your middle name."

"It goes well with his name of Misty." Mace grinned at Kellan. "Misty Drama. It has a certain ring to it."

A cloud formed above Mace when Kellan's eyes filled with mist. "Are you certain of that?"

Danton gave Kellan a pointed look. As soon as the cloud dissipated, he spoke. "Rafe will be awake shortly. He can go with Shade and Livia to the tavern. The rest of you ready yourself to attend the dance. I'll remain here and help Amiel keep an eye on the shop and our prisoner." He glanced at Amiel. "I'm not about to kill him because he won't talk."

Kellan turned to Meikah. "The burgundy dress is on your bed. Along with the dagger."

"We're not going now, are we?" Meikah asked. "It's too early."

Kellan rose from the table. "We need to pay a visit to Tobin. And have a look around the place if we can." He grinned. "It'll make it easier to find our way when we return for the journal."

Meikah nodded, rising to her feet. "It won't take me long to get ready."

"I'll send for the carriage." Kellan grinned. "Before my sister has a chance to request it for collecting her friends this evening."

Chapter Twenty-Four

It took Meikah longer than she expected to get ready. Several times she picked up the night blade dagger, wondering if it would fit in the thigh sheath instead of the normal dagger. In the end, she left it behind. It was too hard to control her magic when she carried night blades. Lightning loved night steel and raced along the dark metal with very little encouragement.

Kellan and Mace waited for her out the front, the carriage parked beside the footpath. Kellan pushed away from the window front of Fable, holding out a hand to Meikah. "You look as amazing as ever."

Meikah smiled as she looked him up and down. Like Mace, he was dressed in evening wear. "You don't look too bad either." She glanced at Mace. "Nor do you."

Kellan handed Meikah inside the carriage. "I was thinking of using the excuse that no one gets to see inside Lord Barnet's place as a reason why we want to be shown around." He sat beside her.

Mace sat across from them. "That should be easy enough. We could also let him think it's part of us taking him along with us."

Meikah looked between each of them as the carriage moved off. "What if he prefers to find his own way there?"

Kellan chuckled. "My parents' servants aren't about to let him in without an invitation."

Meikah couldn't help thinking about all the things that might go wrong. She was still thinking about them when they pulled up out the front of Lord Barnet's mansion. She clambered out of the carriage before anyone had the chance to help her out. Mace and Kellan walked to the front door with her, Mace knocking firmly on the door.

When a servant opened the door, Kellan was the one to speak. "We're here to see Tobin." He slipped past the servant, Mace and Meikah following him. "Is there somewhere we can wait?"

The servant looked from them to the doorway before speaking. "This way." The servant led them to the drawing room Tobin had taken Meikah to earlier that day.

Meikah looked around the room. It was exactly the

same. A shudder went through her as she recalled Tobin's hands on her, his breath against her neck as she pressed the stake against him. At a sound behind her, she turned to face the doorway in time to see Tobin enter. He was dressed in the same clothes as earlier.

"You wish to see me?" Tobin looked at each of them. "Are you going somewhere?"

"My parents are holding a dance this evening," Kellan said. "I assumed you'd be interested in attending as everyone of importance will be there. Including the Duke."

"What time does it begin?" Tobin asked. "Shall I meet you there?"

"We're planning on having dinner at the Duke's Rest beforehand," Kellan said. "We'll take you along to dinner with us and go to my parents' dance afterwards. I wouldn't want our servants to refuse entrance to you."

Tobin glanced down at himself. "I need to dress."

"That's all right," Mace said. "You can have one of the servants show us around the place while you get ready." He grinned. "With how much a recluse Lord Barnet is, no one has seen inside this place in a decade. I'd love to be able to say I have."

"There's no need for you to wait around," Tobin said.

Kellan clapped him on the shoulder. "It's perfectly all right. Take as long as you need to get ready. I'm sure there's plenty for us to see."

"I don't know that Lord Barnet-" Tobin began.

Kellan interrupted him. "It's not like any of you have something to hide. It's a few rooms in a mansion. We're not going to steal the silver." He grinned again. "We have plenty of our own silver. Do you know how much time the servants need to spend keeping it polished? Some of them might quit if I brought more home. They already find it enough of a chore taking care of the ridiculous amount my mother insists we need."

Meikah tried not to smile at how uncomfortable Tobin looked at Kellan's comments.

"I'll call a servant to give you a tour while I get ready. Not that you'll have a chance to see much. It won't take me long to dress. It almost seems pointless." Tobin stepped out of the room returning a moment later with a servant.

The servant remained in the doorway. "If you'd like to follow me."

Meikah started to follow Mace and the servant,

looking over her shoulder when Kellan didn't join them.

Kellan waved her ahead. "I'll catch up with you. There are a couple of questions I want to ask Tobin." Kellan turned to Tobin. "I'm sure you won't mind."

"As you said, we have nothing to hide around here," Tobin said.

Kellan clapped Tobin on the shoulder again. "Very good."

Meikah hurried after the servant and Mace. They were almost out of sight. She caught up to them as they entered another room. The servant showed them around the mansion, answering Mace's many questions. Some of them were about the artwork on the walls, others were about what a room was used for. He asked a mixture of questions so as not to give away the real reason he wanted to know everything about the mansion.

She had no idea how Kellan managed to waylay Tobin for so long, but the servant gave them a full tour of the place before he caught up with them, shrugging when Mace pointed out he'd missed the tour.

Kellan walked beside Meikah as the servant led them back to the drawing room. "I'm sure I'll have the chance to see the place another day. Or evening."

Meikah barely managed to smother her laughter, turning the noise she made into a cough. She gave him a look to let him know she wasn't amused, receiving a grin for her efforts.

Reaching the drawing room, the servant remained in the doorway as they entered. "Can I bring you any refreshments while you wait?"

Mace dropped some coins into the servant's hand. "No, you've been more than helpful. We appreciate you taking so much time to show us around. It's a beautiful place. Lord Barnet must be pleased with the way all of you keep it in such great shape."

The servant bowed. "Thank you, my lord."

Meikah waited until the servant left before speaking softly. "I can't believe the amount of information the servant gave us."

Before either of them had a chance to reply, Tobin entered the drawing room, dressed in evening wear. "Should we leave now? It's probably well and truly around dinner time." He sent Kellan a look of annoyance when he spoke the last few words.

"It's the perfect time for dinner." Kellan offered his arm to Meikah. "Shall we?"

She rested a hand on his arm walking with him out to the carriage, Mace and Tobin following.

Kellan and Mace kept the conversation going on

the way to the tavern. Tobin barely said a word. Neither did Meikah. Reaching the Duke's Rest, a table was quickly found for them and their meal orders were taken. Kellan and Mace continued to keep the conversation going.

Meikah looked around the tavern. It was fairly crowded and noisy, which didn't surprise her in the least considering what time it was. There were a few people she recognised, mainly friends of her grandparents. At least there'd be no reason for them to run to Harlen and Sirena with tales. Meikah glanced at Kellan. Or at least not as far as she knew. Knowing Kellan, that situation could change at any moment.

The meal was uneventful and Kellan led the way back to the carriage that awaited them out the front. It was a short journey to Kellan's place, but they were unable to pull up directly out the front due to all the other carriages lined up beside the footpath.

Kellan tapped on the roof. "No need to try and get any closer. Here will do." Kellan swung the door open, helping Meikah out before he followed her onto the footpath.

The coachman spoke before they'd gone far. "Do I need to remind you of your parents' wishes, my lord?"

Looking over his shoulder, Kellan grinned. "Do you think it'd help?"

"I doubt it, my lord," the coachman said dryly.

"I won't need you again this evening," Kellan said. When the coachman nodded, Kellan led the way to the front door.

Chapter Twenty-Five

Meikah stared at everything as they entered the mansion. It was the first time she'd been in Kellan's home. It was as opulent as the other mansions she'd visited recently. And probably more crowded than both of Lady Eris' events.

Kellan led the way to where his parents greeted their guests. "Mother, Father, this is Meikah." He turned to Meikah. "My parents Tertia and Powel."

Meikah curtsied. "Lady Tertia. Lord Powel." Both his parents had the same coloured black hair as Kellan and his mother had brown eyes the same colour as Kellan's while his father's eyes were hazel. Both were dressed in the latest fashions and Lady Tertia wore a fortune in jewels.

Tertia inclined her head, while Powel nodded politely, both greeting Mace, before Powel turned to his son. "Should we be concerned you decided to join us this evening?"

Kellan grinned. "I thought you were perpetually concerned." He gestured towards Tobin. "Tobin and his father are staying with Lord Barnet."

Kellan's father again nodded before returning his attention to his son. "Try not to enjoy yourself too much this evening." He emphasised the word 'too'.

Chuckling, Kellan led the way further into the mansion. When they reached the ballroom, he turned to Meikah. "Would you like to dance?"

Tobin interrupted before Meikah could say anything. "I thought you said the Duke would be here this evening."

Kellan held his hand out to Meikah, glancing at Tobin. "He'll turn up when he's ready."

Meikah took Kellan's hand. "I'd love to dance."

Mace interrupted Tobin, who started to protest. "There are some people I'd like you to meet." Mace led the protesting Tobin away.

Meikah allowed Kellan to lead her out amongst the guests who were dancing. When the dance brought them together, she asked, "Who is Mace introducing Tobin to?"

Kellan grinned, the dance moving them apart. When they were close again, Kellan said, "Some of the gossips. After they finish interrogating him he's probably going to really hate Mace."

Meikah returned Kellan's grin. She couldn't feel much sympathy for Tobin. At least not in this instance. She waited for the dance to bring them close again so she could speak. "When are we leaving?"

"In a few hours. It'll give everyone at Lord Barnet's mansion time to go to sleep. Luckily they're accustomed to retiring early."

Once again Meikah had to wait until the dance brought them together before she could speak. "You weren't with us when the servant told us that information. How do you know?"

Kellan waited until the dance brought them together. "I didn't spend all the time keeping Tobin distracted. While looking for the two of you I managed to make a lot of interesting discoveries on my own."

The dance ended, followed by one that kept them close to each other. "What sort of things?" Meikah asked.

Kellan only smiled. "Bring you to a dance and all you want to do is work."

"Probably because that's the only time you take me to a dance," Meikah said.

Kellan spun her around on the dance floor. "I'll have to fix that problem."

The evening passed quicker than Meikah expected. She also danced with a few young men Kellan introduced her to. When the Duke arrived, Mace brought Tobin back to them.

Kellan grinned before he introduced Tobin to the Duke. "I'd like you to meet Tobin, Your Grace. He's new to Dreyton so I'm sure there are a lot of things he could tell you that you haven't already heard from the rest of us. Why I'm sure he could probably keep you entertained for an hour or two."

"That'd be a nice change from hearing about your latest exploit," the Duke said dryly. He turned to Tobin. "Where are you from, Tobin, wasn't it?"

Kellan tugged Meikah away from the Duke, leaning close to speak to her. "Time to go." He led the way to his room, taking out an outfit for each of them from the chest of drawers sitting against the wall opposite his bed. A bewitched flame lantern sat atop the drawers.

Mace, who followed her, closed the bedroom door as he entered and took a navy coloured outfit from Kellan.

Meikah took an outfit too. "When did you bring these here?" She glanced around the room. It was bigger than her room, the large bed dominating one end of the room, a long chest across the foot of it. There was a fireplace in the wall opposite the door, curtains that went to the floor on either side of it, both well away from it. Another door led from the room to the right, on the same wall the chest of drawers was against. It led into a room filled with hanging clothes. Shoes and boots were lined up beneath them.

Kellan grinned. "I asked Danton if he could organise it. He also made sure our weapons were brought over." He handed Meikah's night steel weapons to her.

"Where will I get changed?" Meikah took the weapons, glad she'd have them with her. Who knew what they'd face.

Kellan nodded towards his dressing room as he handed over Mace's weapons. "There is a curtain you can pull across the doorway and a bewitched flame lamp on the left as you enter."

"Thank you." Meikah hurried inside the dressing room and pulled the curtain, turning on the lamp. She placed the clothes and weapons on the chest of drawers the lamp sat on, stripping off the gown she wore. It didn't take her long to change into the Assassins Of The Dead outfit, along with her weapons, and pull on the full face mask. Pushing aside the curtain, she stepped into the room, looking away when she realised Kellan and Mace were dressing. "Sorry."

Kellan chuckled. "You were quicker than we thought you'd be."

She kept her gaze averted. "What do I do with my gown?"

"Leave it in the dressing room. I'll see that it's returned to you later," Kellan said. "You can look now."

Mace chuckled. "If he's lucky he'll do something with the gown before the servants comment to his parents about it being left there."

Kellan crossed the room, pulling on his full face mask. "I think they're at the point where nothing surprises them anymore." He opened the curtain on the right, revealing a glass paned door that led onto a balcony.

"Where are we going?" Meikah followed him, peering outside.

Kellan laughed. "Exactly where you think. Over the side."

Mace joined her, also wearing a full face mask with his outfit. "It isn't as bad as it looks. There are plenty of handholds. You'll easily reach the ground."

Stepping onto the balcony, Meikah looked over the edge. The ground was only one storey away, not too bad should she lose her footing. She stepped back, turning to Kellan. "Lead the way."

Mace chuckled. "Are you hoping he'll catch you if you fall?"

"You better be right and it's easy so there is no possibility of me falling," Meikah warned.

Kellan slipped over the side of the balcony. "I've arranged for horses to be waiting. They'll be outside the stable." He climbed down the wall of the mansion, dropping to the ground when he was close.

Meikah followed, relieved to find Mace was right. The climb down was easier than it looked. Reaching the ground, she followed Kellan around the building to where three horses were tied up at the front of a stable. "Won't someone recognise the horses?"

"They're not my parents' horses." Kellan swung into the saddle.

"Who do they belong to?" Meikah took the reins of one of the horses, swinging into the saddle.

"Danton." Kellan urged his horse into a walk.

Meikah followed, glancing at Mace who rode alongside her. "Where are we going to leave them while we're breaking into Lord Barnet's mansion?"

Kellan chuckled as she came alongside him.

"There's always somewhere to leave a horse when you're in the wealthier neighbourhoods."

Guessing he wasn't going to explain further, Meikah fell silent, continuing to remain beside Kellan as he headed towards Lord Barnet's place. They found a place behind the stable to leave their horses, a fenced yard that contained several other horses.

Chapter Twenty-Six

The mansion and its surrounds were quiet and Meikah silently followed Kellan, Mace behind her. Excitement raced through her when she was able to see in the dark so she could find her way towards the mansion. It wasn't as bright as day, but more than sufficient to get where she needed to go. Amiel was a much better teacher than the sorcerer had been.

Kellan moved slowly along the back of the mansion, stopping regularly to look upwards. Eventually, he scaled the wall and swung himself onto a balcony, Mace following.

Meikah took a deep breath before she did the same. It was more difficult than climbing down the wall of Kellan's place, but easier than she'd thought it would be. Pulling herself onto the balcony to stand with Kellan and Mace, she waited for Kellan to remove the wards so they could enter. "What is taking so long?" She leaned close so she could keep her voice low.

"Whoever his sorcerer is, they know what they're doing." Kellan spoke equally quiet.

"Does that mean you won't be able to get past the wards?" Meikah asked.

Kellan laughed softly. "I haven't come across a ward I can't remove. Or set again. You might say it's one of my talents."

Mace leaned in close. "Certainly not your main talent. That'd be getting into trouble."

Before Meikah could ask him if he'd discovered the one ward he couldn't remove, he opened the door, briefly looking over his shoulder. She followed him inside, staying close and being as quiet as possible. The place was dark and silent. No one seemed to be awake. She paused in the doorway, looking in both directions like Kellan did. It was deserted.

They crept along the hallway, headed towards the sitting room where Lord Hemmet frequently left his journal. She had no idea how they'd manage to take it if it was in his bedroom with him. When Kellan stopped at the doorway to the sitting room, she peered inside. The room was in darkness, only her magic allowing her to see the sparsely furnished room. Her gaze was drawn to the small timber table beside an armchair. A smile formed. Lord Hemmet had left his journal behind.

She hurried into the sitting room, following Kellan, Mace remaining close behind her. When Kellan picked up the journal she rested a hand on it when he was about to tuck it away. "Are we sure it's his journal?"

Kellan opened to the last page, a ribbon marking the place. He read out the words, his voice soft. "I see them in my dreams of a night. My nightmares. All my family. Their lifeless, blood drained bodies, sightless eyes staring accusingly up at me. It seems wrong that only I should have survived. As in life, I am unable to do anything to help as they're slaughtered in front of me, night after night."

"That sounds like it to me," Mace said.

Kellan tucked it away. "Let's get this to Danton." He started for the doorway.

Meikah drew him back when she heard a sound. "What was that?"

No one had a chance to answer before they heard someone muttering as they came towards them. "Don't touch it. Bring it to me. Leave it where I left it. Why isn't it here waiting for me? Can't please some folk."

Meikah glanced around the room, looking for

somewhere to hide. She hurried towards the curtain that hung in front of the window. It went to the floor. She slipped behind it, Kellan and Mace joining her. "We take up too much space." She peered around the edge of the curtain. The servant, who Lord Hemmet had abused earlier, entered. He carried a candle, shielding it so it didn't go out.

"We'll go out the window," Kellan whispered.

She glanced at Kellan. "Stop moving. You're shifting the curtain." She peered around the edge of the curtain again.

The servant was searching on the floor under the small table. "Where did he leave it now?" The servant struggled to his feet, placing the candle on the table as he searched the armchair, slipping his hands down the side and under the cushion. He continued to mutter about Lord Hemmet.

Feeling a draft behind her Meikah turned to see Kellan had the window open. She wanted to protest when he climbed out and headed to the right, the curtains shifting. She shook her head when Mace indicated she should go next.

"Where's that draft coming from?" the servant muttered. "I'll be glad for the day when they go."

A peek around the edge of the curtain showed the servant picked up the candle then started towards the window. Meikah didn't continue to watch. She clambered out the window to find that Kellan and Mace inched their way along a ledge. Both were now heading towards the left, Mace leading the way.

After looking down below, she pressed her back against the wall. The drop wasn't overly high, but landing on the paved path below would probably break a bone or two. She caught up with Kellan and Mace who'd stopped at the next window.

"It's locked from the inside." Kellan kept his voice low. "We'll have to see if the next window is unlocked."

She continued to follow them along the building as they checked each of the windows. The corner of the building came closer. Meikah began to wonder what they were going to do. They couldn't jump. She glanced up. And that wasn't an option either. She had no idea if it would be possible to go around the corner of the building and breaking a window was sure to catch someone's attention.

Mace reached the corner and peered around it, clutching the edge of the building and leaning at an awkward angle as he did so. "The ledge continues. Eventually."

"We'll fall." Meikah looked at the rose bushes

below. They wouldn't be any better to land on than the pavers.

"I think I can see an open window along this side," Mace said.

Kellan pressed himself firmly against the wall and grabbed Mace's arm. "I'll keep you steady."

Mace stretched out around the corner, Kellan keeping hold of his arm.

Meikah remained pressed against the wall, her breath held as she watched Mace slowly move around the corner of the building. Once he was around, Kellan beckoned her closer. When she was next to Kellan, she saw the ledge didn't go quite to the end of the building. Mace's earlier comment now made sense. "I can't do that."

"Of course you can." Kellan eased around the corner, Mace gripping hold of his arm.

Meikah went as close to the edge as possible. She eyed the gap between the ledge and the end of the building. If it was the same on the other side, there was absolutely no way she could manage. Her legs weren't as long as theirs.

Kellan peered around the edge of the building. "I'll hold your arm and help steady you."

Meikah shook her head. "I can't."

"You don't have many options. You can go back

and smash a window, but somebody will hear you. You can jump to the ground below, but there are two rose bushes down there that will break your fall in the wrong kind of way. And I don't think there's any way of climbing up the building," Kellan said.

She closed her eyes for a moment, leaning against the building. The options sounded worse spoken aloud and she could think of no other choices. Moving as far as possible along the ledge, she stretched out her arm and waited until Kellan took hold of it before she tried to get around the corner. There was nothing. She stretched out her foot as far as she could, but still couldn't find the ledge on the other side.

"Another six inches," Kellan said.

She stretched out a little more, but knew it wasn't enough. "I–"

Kellan interrupted her. "You have to. You can't stay here all night."

Again she momentarily closed her eyes, taking a deep breath before she stretched a little further. The tips of her toes felt something.

"That's it," Kellan said. "A little further."

"What are you doing out there?" a voice behind Meikah demanded.

"Hurry," Kellan said. "Mace has reached the open window."

She slid her toes further along the ledge, her limbs aching at how much she pushed them to stretch further.

"I'm fetching the dogs," the servant warned.

Chapter Twenty-Seven

Meikah's foot was finally fully on the ledge and she was able to join Kellan on the other side. She remained pressed against the wall a moment before she could bring herself to move, ignoring Kellan urging her to go.

"There's movement inside," Mace called softly out the window.

"We have to go," Kellan said.

Taking a deep breath, Meikah continued along the building, climbing in the window after Kellan. Not that it helped. They couldn't go anywhere while footsteps ran past the closed door of the empty bedroom. "What are we going to do?" She kept her voice as low as possible.

Kellan crossed the room, not answering. He pressed his ear against the door, eventually opening it to peer out. He beckoned them forward, leading them through the mansion, having to backtrack twice and hide in an empty room once.

They slipped outside, the sound of dogs in the distance. Mace broke into a run, heading towards where they'd left the horses. They reached the horses before the dogs came close, riding away from the mansion. Meikah kept looking over her shoulder, but no one followed them through the streets. They slowed as they neared the main road. She would have preferred to speed up rather than slow down. But it would draw too much attention if they galloped along the main road.

Once more Meikah looked over her shoulder. "I kept expecting them to follow." She looked over her shoulder again as they turned onto the main road.

Kellan chuckled. "I don't think the household is that organised." As they neared Fable, he headed around the back, tying his horse to the hitching post once he'd dismounted.

Meikah did the same, following him inside to where Danton sat at the kitchen table, talking to Amiel who stood in the hallway doorway. Both fell silent as the three of them entered.

Danton rose to his feet, taking the journal Kellan held out. "Did you have any trouble getting it?"

Kellan glanced at Meikah. "Getting it was no trouble at all."

She was almost certain Kellan was grinning beneath his full face mask. "What did Livia, Shade and Rafe learn?"

"They haven't returned," Danton said.

"Should they have returned by now?" Meikah asked.

Danton turned to Mace. "I need you to stay here with Amiel and help him watch the shop and the prisoner. I need to see a couple of people and get things ready in case we need to call on the Duke's men." He turned to Kellan and Meikah. "I want the two of you to ride out to the tavern and see what you can learn. Don't get caught and return if it's more than you can handle."

Kellan slung an arm around Meikah's shoulders. "We'll be fine." Keeping his arm around her, he strode to the back door, letting go of her before heading outside.

She swung into the saddle, riding alongside Kellan. "How will we find them? Neither of us has the ability to track like Livia or Rafe can."

"We'll find them," Kellan stated.

She could only hope he was right. But what if something had happened? Images of how crowded the tavern had been came to mind. What if they'd been overwhelmed by the members of the Society Against Vampires? The entire ride to the Dancing Duck, Meikah kept thinking over all the things that might have gone wrong. There were so many of them.

As they approached, Kellan circled around the tavern, remaining in the forest. They found a single horse. "This is Shade's horse. We'll leave ours with it and see if we can find where they went."

Meikah dismounted, tying the reins to a branch, her magic helping her see in the dark. She glanced around the area, seeing no sign of anyone. "How are we going to find them?"

Kellan chuckled. "Stumble on them?"

She glared at him even though he was already walking off. She hurried after him. "That's a terrible plan."

"Have you got a better one?" Kellan stopped at the edge of the treeline, peering around a tree.

She joined him. "No." There were two men patrolling the area behind the tavern. "How are we meant to get past them?"

"Create a diversion."

Again she glared at him. "I want to go inside, not get caught."

"We won't be caught." Kellan chuckled as one of the men spun around, rubbing at his neck.

"What did you do to him?"

"Fog across the back of his neck."

She grinned when the man kept moving further away. "What about the second one?"

"Give me a chance," Kellan said.

The second man rubbed the back of his neck, striding towards the first man. "What are you doing?"

"Nothing. What do you think you're doing?" the first man demanded.

The second man glanced around the area. "Someone must be out there messing with us." He pointed in Meikah and Kellan's direction. "You check over there and I'll check here." He headed in the opposite direction.

Kellan grabbed Meikah's hand, tugging her to the side. Once they were across from the side of the tavern, he ran for the corner of the building.

Meikah ran with him, her grip tightening on his as she tried to keep her steps light. They pressed themselves against the wall when they reached it. She followed him to the corner which he peered around before tugging her with him to the back of the building, creeping along the wall until they reached the door. Over near the edge of the forest, she heard the two men call out to each other, asking if either had found anything. They continued to search and she frequently glanced at them, worried they'd return to where they'd been before and spot them.

Kellan eased the door open, slipping inside after checking through the gap, tugging Meikah with him.

She scanned inside the tavern, the place quiet and deserted. A fire burned low in a fireplace not far from the bar, but that was the only movement. Closing the door behind her, she kept hold of Kellan's hand, following him across the room to the stairs. "Where is everyone? It's a tavern. Shouldn't there be a few people here?"

"Not at this hour." Kellan let go of her hand to lift the trapdoor slightly.

Before he could fully open it, a bat landed beside them, becoming Rafe. "The other two are stuck upstairs. We retreated up there when someone came in earlier. Now the people are in the hallway talking and the other two are hiding in one of the rooms, waiting for them to leave."

"Should we create a distraction?" Meikah asked.

Rafe gestured towards the trapdoor Kellan had closed at his arrival. "While they're upstairs, we can see who is in here."

With a nod, Kellan bent to open the trapdoor again. He peered inside, the soft glow of light from the room below falling across him. "There are people chained up down there."

"People or vampires?" Rafe asked.

"Vampires." Kellan pushed the trapdoor wide open. "There doesn't seem to be any guards."

Chapter Twenty-Eight

Meikah crouched beside Kellan to peer into the basement. "How are we going to get them out of the tavern without being seen?" Wooden stairs led into the basement, one side of them running down a rock wall, the other side open, not even a railing. She leaned in to see the far side, a variety of weapons, barrels and chests off to her left. Before she could see the other end, Kellan drew her back from the edge.

"Don't fall down there," Kellan said.

"I don't care if we're seen escaping," Rafe said. "I'm not leaving them behind."

Letting go of Meikah, Kellan turned to Rafe. "You have a look around and see how many are in the area. Other than the ones in the hallway and the two out the back. We might need to return to Fable for help if there are too many. Or have the boss send for the Duke's men."

"You can't let him go off on his own," Meikah protested.

"It's night. A bat wouldn't be out of place," Kellan said.

"They won't spot me." Rafe became a bat and flew upstairs.

"I'll go first. You follow." Kellan started down the wooden steps.

Meikah grabbed his arm before he'd reached the third one. "This feels like walking into a trap. It only has one exit."

Kellan moved her hand from his arm, linking his fingers through hers. "Others know where we are. Do you think Inferno would leave us behind when he won't leave behind strangers?" Kellan nodded towards the basement, using the name Danton had given Rafe for when he was incognito.

"What if he's caught?"

Kellan lightly squeezed her hand. "If none of us returned, the boss would come after us."

"Everyone else was late returning and he didn't go after them," Meikah said.

"He would have if the three of us weren't on the way back." Kellan paused a moment. "Did you want to wait upstairs while I go into the basement?"

She didn't like that idea any better. "We'll go together."

Kellan took a step forward. "Look out for traps. Don't put your weight on each step until you test it first."

Meikah did as he recommended, examining each step for a trap before carefully placing her foot down. Reaching the bottom of the steps, she scanned the area. At the other end of the basement were five vampires with chains around their ankles, the other end attached to the rock wall. They were bruised and injured, blood smeared across them and staining the floor.

One of the vampires raised his head to stare up at them, remaining sprawled on the floor. "Haven't you already done enough tonight? Was this part of your game? Let us think we're safe for the night then return to put us through it all over again."

Meikah started forward, wanting to help.

Kellan drew her back. "They're vampires that have lost a lot of blood."

Meikah gestured towards them. "We can't leave them here. We have to help them escape."

"You should listen to him," the vampire said. "I've never killed a human yet, but I don't know how I'd be able to stop if I started to drink your blood. If you've truly come to rescue us, I wouldn't want to repay you in that way."

One of the other vampires stirred, their mumbled words incoherent.

The other vampire glanced at them. "The rest are worse. But at least we survived another night. There's always one who doesn't." He pointed to the vampire in the corner. "He's been with them a month. They brought him with them. By morning, they'll have found another vampire to replace the one who didn't survive this night."

Meikah frowned. "I don't understand what you're talking about."

The vampire met her gaze. "They torture us. The first vampire to make a sound, dies."

Shock raced through her. The words seemed worse with the bland tone he used. "They…" She couldn't get the rest of the words out.

"You really are here to rescue us," the vampire said.

Kellan nodded, turning to Meikah. "Go up to the bar and find a cup we can put some blood in. If we take the edge off their hunger, it should help."

She wanted to beg him to come with her. What if she ran into one of the members of the Society Against Vampires? Drawing in a slow, deep breath she headed up the stairs, once again testing them before she put her full weight on each one. Who knew how traps worked. She certainly didn't.

Behind the bar, she found a tin cup, dinted and scratched, but seeming to be fairly clean. She started towards the trapdoor, freezing when the front door opened and a man stepped inside, closing the door behind him.

Turning in her direction, the man drew a sword, opening his mouth.

Worried he'd call for help, Meikah raised her hand, about to warn him to be silent or she'd attack. A lightning dragon struck him, knocking him down, his sword clattering across the floor. Meikah winced. Had anyone heard? She ran forward, gathering up the sword, still holding the cup in her left hand. She spun at a sound, expecting it to be one of the people from upstairs.

Kellan came out of the trapdoor, hurrying forward when he saw the man sprawled on the floor. He hoisted him over his shoulder, looking upstairs at the sound of footsteps.

"I think someone heard." Meikah kept her voice low as she followed Kellan back to the trapdoor.

"Seems that way. Shut the trapdoor behind us." Kellan headed down the stairs, dropping the man in a heap beside them.

"What if they check down here?" Meikah went down the stairs more quickly this time. Surely if there were any traps, they would have found them by now.

The vampire struggled to rise to his feet. "Let me have him. He's nothing to you and he stood by and watched while we were tortured, sometimes taking his turn."

Kellan took the cup from Meikah, making a small cut in the unconscious man's arm. He held the arm over the tin cup. "We won't let you kill him. We'll see that he pays for his crimes, but not that way."

"Who are you?" the vampire asked.

Kellan held the tin cup out to Meikah. "Give this to him while I bind up the cut. We wouldn't want him bleeding to death." He looked towards the vampire as he tore a piece of cloth from the unconscious man's sleeve. "We're here on business for the King."

The vampire took the cup that Meikah pushed closer to him, stretched out as far as she could without coming too close. "The King knows?" He raised the cup to his lips.

"The King's people are everywhere, carrying out his business and seeing to it that lawbreakers pay for their crimes." Kellan rose to his feet. "Is it safe to approach you?"

Before the vampire could answer, there was a

scratching at the trapdoor. Meikah hurried up the steps and opened it slightly. A bat flew in and landed on the floor, becoming Rafe. He gestured towards the trapdoor. "Close it."

"How many are up there?" Kellan asked.

"One of them rode to town," Rafe said. "Midnight jumped out the upstairs window. She said she was going to let the boss know. I told her about the prisoners. We can't set them free. She said the boss will send the Duke's men. They'll need to be here for them to find."

"You'd leave us here for them to kill us?" the vampire demanded.

Rafe took the empty tin cup from the vampire, stepping back out of his way. "They're out the back. All we have to do is keep them busy until the Duke's men get here." He picked up the unconscious man and threw him over his shoulder. "Someone want to open the trapdoor?"

Meikah hurried up the stairs. Opening the trapdoor, she found Shade keeping watch at the back door. She hurried forward. "What's happening?"

Shade nodded towards the front door. "We barricaded the front door and shoved tables against the windows. The only way in is through the back. Looks like they're preparing to enter."

Meikah scanned the tavern. The place was a mess. Chairs had been knocked over and some of them were jammed behind the tables barricading the front door and windows. "Are we staying in here?"

Kellan joined Meikah and Shade at the window. "Inferno is putting the man you knocked out in a bed upstairs." He chuckled. "One less problem to explain. At least until he wakes up and tries to argue he's innocent."

Chapter Twenty-Nine

Meikah stared at the armed men and women behind the tavern. They spoke quietly amongst themselves, several of them nodding. She wished she had hearing as good as Rafe's so she knew what to expect. "What's our plan?"

Rafe joined them at the window. "They're about to attack. You better decide quickly."

"We keep them busy and try not to kill them. When the Duke's men arrive, move in close as I'll bring a heavy fog to cover our retreat. If we don't stay together, we'll get separated." Kellan drew his sword and dagger, glancing around the group. "Everyone ready?"

Nodding, Meikah drew her sword and dagger.

Shade drew a dagger. "I'll get the door." He glanced at Rafe. "Try not to let them realise you're a vampire. The less they know about us, the better." He swung the door open.

Rafe was out the door first, Kellan following him. Meikah followed behind Shade. She tried not to think about how outnumbered they were. The numerous weapons held ready and the sea of faces in front of her made it a little hard to ignore. How long would it take for the Duke's men to arrive?

The members of the Society Against Vampires attacked, many of them making threatening comments. Rafe attacked at a slower pace than usual and flames flickered along the blades of his daggers. Lightning crawled along Meikah's blades. The flames hadn't caused the crowd to pause, but the lightning did.

Not that it slowed them for long. Meikah blocked the sword aimed at her. She barely managed to avoid being struck by a battleaxe. It was a lot easier when you didn't have to keep your opponent alive. Especially when they were trying to kill you. Meikah blocked and attacked as she listened for approaching help. Time dragged out, help not seeming to arrive. She had no idea how long they could keep this up. Already her arms tired from blocking the attacks from some of the larger weapons.

When she finally heard approaching horses,

Meikah tried to tell herself she only had a little longer to last. Dread washed over her when the newcomers rode around the side of the tavern. It wasn't the Duke's men.

"Retreat," Kellan ordered.

"We can't leave-" Rafe began.

Kellan interrupted. "Retreat. Now."

Meikah wanted to protest too. Surely they weren't going to leave the captives behind. She slowly backed away towards the forest with the rest of her companions.

"This isn't right," Rafe said. "We should be-" he broke off. "More are coming."

Again Meikah wanted to protest. There were already too many for them to face. They needed to be running, not just retreating. What had made them think they could face the crowd she'd seen in the tavern when Tobin had taken her there? She continued to back up, the crowd following, waiting for the newcomers to join them, laughing at how outnumbered Meikah and her companions were.

A black mountain cat leapt out of the forest, landing between the two groups, snarling. Several members of the crowd stumbled back. A few others told them to hold their ground, they still outnumbered them.

Livia snarled again, prowling back and forth, moving closer to Kellan as she did.

"Move in close," Kellan ordered.

Remembering his earlier plan, Meikah moved close to Kellan, sheathing her dagger so she could wrap her hand around his upper arm. Even with Livia's help, they were still outnumbered. She'd barely taken hold of his arm, when fog rose up around them.

"Don't let them escape," one of the men called out. He was echoed by several others.

Sheathing her sword, Meikah moved into the forest with Kellan, Rafe's hand slipping into hers. She kept her voice low, not wanting the crowd to hear where they'd gone. "What are we going to do about the vampires? Can we circle around and set them free?" She refused to leave innocent men behind.

"The Duke's men are nearly here," Livia said from beside Meikah.

She was startled to hear Livia speak, having thought the shapeshifter was still in animal form. "They'll be safe?" It was hard to believe after the earlier shock at the arrival of more members of the Society Against Vampires.

"Safer than us," Shade said. "Now be quiet so the crowd can't find us."

They remained amongst the trees, making their

way towards where the horses had been left, the sound of the searchers following them. The sounds changed, hoofbeats drowning out the calls of the searchers. The sounds of the searchers were quickly replaced by the Duke's men calling out for the crowd to put down their weapons. The fog dissipated.

It took Meikah a second to realise that somehow they'd lasted long enough. The Duke's men would take care of the members of the Society Against Vampires and rescue the vampires in the basement. No more innocent vampires would die.

"About time they arrived," Livia said. "I didn't leave them that far behind."

Mounting the horse, Meikah looked in the direction of the tavern, even though she couldn't see it through the trees. The sound of fighting reached her. At least some of the Society Against Vampires weren't going to give up without a fight. "Should we stay and help the Duke's men?"

"They outnumber SAV. It won't take them long to subdue SAV and the vampires will be freed." Livia shifted into her cat form, running ahead. Shade rode after her.

Meikah followed Kellan who rode at a slower pace, Rafe taking bat form to fly above them. "We're no longer needed?"

"The Duke's men will take care of everything. It's better this way," Kellan assured her. "Time to return to the shop." He urged the horse into a canter, not slowing until they approached Dreyton.

They left the horses behind Fable, heading inside to find Danton seated at the table, the journal open in front of him. He looked up when they entered. "It isn't Hemmet. He wrote that all his family were killed and when he sought out the vampires who killed them, he saved their prisoners, including a boy who reminded him of his son. A boy who'd been with the vampires so long, and from such a young age, he'd forgotten the name his family had once given him."

"Tobin isn't his son?" Meikah asked.

"It's worse than that," Danton said.

Meikah frowned, trying to make sense of his comment. "What do you mean by worse?"

"Tobin is one of the leaders of SAV. They joined together, but when Hemmet became disgusted by the methods they began to use, Tobin rose in the ranks by outdoing them. Hemmet wants them to return to their earlier methods." Danton closed the journal. "There's enough information in here that my brother will want to send it on to the King once he's finished reading it. There are two other groups that have been started. One in the capital and one in the Arcton Mountains."

Mace burst into the kitchen. "The Duke sent a message to say Tobin is no longer at Kellan's parents' place. He left at some stage after his men were given the order to round up all those watching him and to go after the prisoners since now there was proof."

"We can't let him escape," Meikah said.

"We don't know where he'll go." Livia stood beside Shade, an arm around his waist, his arm around her shoulders.

Meikah smiled. "I do. The Arcton Mountains. A place filled with vampires. Somewhere he's been before and would probably be welcomed back. Somewhere that he'd like to rid of vampires."

"There's only one road he'd take." Kellan strode towards the back door.

"I'm going too." Meikah followed him.

Livia hurried after them. "I'm not about to be left behind."

"All of you go," Danton said. "In case he has people with him. I need to deliver the journal and the prisoner in the basement to my brother. Amiel can look after the place since I won't be long. And I doubt anyone else should arrive looking for help now SAV is being rounded up." He strode towards the hallway, pausing to look over his shoulder before he left the kitchen. "Don't get caught."

Chapter Thirty

Meikah smiled at Danton's familiar words, stepping outside to collect the horse she'd ridden earlier, Kellan and Mace already on their horses. She swung into the saddle. "What if he's staying low until daylight?"

"I'll go ahead and see if I can spot him on the road." Rafe became a bat, flying off into the night.

Meikah remained with the rest of them, Livia seated behind Shade, all of them keeping their horses to a walk so as not to draw unwanted attention.

Rafe met them as they were leaving Dreyton, landing ahead of them on the road and shifting to his vampire form. "He's ahead of us. Alone."

They urged their horses into a gallop, quickly catching up to Tobin. They surrounded him. His hand rested on the sword at his side. "What do you want?"

"To take you back to Dreyton to answer for your

crimes against innocent vampires." Kellan spoke in a deeper voice than usual, not sounding like himself, his mask also helping to hide his identity.

The voice Kellan used reminded Meikah they needed to keep Tobin from learning who they were. The words she'd been about to speak remained unspoken and she was glad she'd left her mask on.

"Don't you understand? I'm doing you a favour. They'll enslave every one of us eventually." Tobin dismounted, drawing his sword. "I will never be enslaved again." He swung at Kellan, who was still on his horse.

The animal reared back, Kellan leaping from its back the moment all four feet were on the ground again. He drew his sword and dagger, joining Rafe who was already attacking Tobin.

Meikah dismounted, along with the rest of her companions. She didn't have the chance to draw her weapons before Tobin slammed his sword into the ground, a rush of air forcing all of them backwards. Meikah struggled to keep her feet.

"It's been spelled," Kellan warned. "With more than one spell judging by the amount of writing on it."

Meikah drew her weapons, remaining back as she warily watched Tobin.

He drew his sword from the ground, grinning at them. "Not expecting that, were you?" He attacked again, focusing on Kellan and Livia.

Meikah drew near, watching for an opportunity to attack. This time, when Tobin raised the sword above his head, lightning streaked out from it. Meikah threw herself forward, dropping her sword as she held up her hand to protect her companions. The lightning didn't get the chance to strike her hand. The lacey dragon collided with it, the impact throwing Tobin off his feet. She lowered her hand, staring at it for a moment before she turned her attention to Tobin.

He stared up at her, dazed. "What are you?"

She grinned, even though he wouldn't be able to see it through the mask. On either side of her were Kellan and Rafe, the rest of her companions standing around them. She disguised her voice before she spoke, using as low a tone as possible. "An Assassin Of The Dead."

Livia pointed Tobin's own sword at him. "You picked the wrong town this time."

Meikah's grin remained in place as Kellan and Shade dragged Tobin to his feet, tying him up before slinging him over the back of his horse. He certainly had chosen the wrong town. Her gaze was once again drawn to her hand. She'd had no idea what she'd planned to do earlier, only having fleetingly thought that lightning might have been able to beat lightning. The lacey dragon had been unexpected. She looked in the direction of the Arcton Mountains. She didn't want to return to them, but maybe she needed to so she could find a dragon to answer some of her many questions.

Livia swung up behind Shade, looking at Meikah. "Are you coming?"

With one last glance towards the mountains, she nodded.

It was nearly morning by the time everything was sorted, including learning the prisoners had been freed and that one of them was the missing husband of the first vampire that had come to them looking for help. The second vampire hadn't been so lucky. They'd also learned that Tobin had been planning to assassinate the Duke in an attempt to have a ruler in Dreyton who wasn't sympathetic to vampires.

Meikah dressed in her usual clothes, alternating between staying at Fable or going home. Surely after all Amiel had taught her, especially that of letting some of the magic go rather than forcing it all down so it exploded, she could manage not to hurt her family. By the time she made up her mind, the sun was beginning to rise and only Kellan was around to walk her home.

"Who is going to walk you back?" Meikah stood by the front door of Fable, blocking Kellan's way.

"Dreyton is safe again," Kellan said.

"Then why do you need to walk me home?"

Kellan took hold of her hand, grinning. "Do I need an excuse? I could probably come up with one, but what's wrong with wanting to take an early morning stroll with you?"

She eyed him up and down, trying to figure out if he was planning something. It was impossible to tell. In the end, she let him walk her home. During the walk, she decided she should go in the front door rather than sneak in her window. She stopped not far from the door, turning to face Kellan. Before she could speak, he did.

"I'll see you tomorrow night." Letting go of her hand, he strolled away.

She glared at his retreating figure, having wanted to ask him what was happening the next night. And why wouldn't she be seeing him later today? She was going to train with Amiel in the afternoon. But he'd been too quick for her. What was he planning? Mentally shrugging, she faced the door, which she discovered was locked, needing a moment before she could bring herself to knock.

The door swung open nearly a minute later, Heron in the doorway. "You finally decided to come home."

"I'm sorry about-"

Heron interrupted, stepping back. "Inside. Breena has been waiting to see you. My father is here too. We were trying to figure out what to do about the parcel that was delivered for you half an hour ago."

"Parcel?" She followed Heron inside and to the dining table where a lined box sat open, a ballgown clearly visible. "That was addressed to me?"

Breena came forward, throwing her arms around Meikah and holding her tight. "Don't ever do that again."

Before Meikah could apologise for attacking her father, Breena continued to speak.

"We were so worried. You don't run away. You stay and deal with the problem."

Meikah guessed this wasn't the time to point out that they were the ones who'd wanted her to run away. Or at least leave town until the gossip died down. Returning Breena's hug, she eventually pulled away. "Who is it from?" She glanced at the ballgown.

Harlen held out a gold-edged invitation. "You can't turn it down."

She stared at the words. "The Duke and Duchess have invited me to their ball tomorrow evening?"

"She isn't going," Heron stated. "Kellan is sure to be there. She isn't to have anything more to do with him."

Meikah took the invitation from her grandfather, smiling as Kellan's words made sense. "I need a sleep." She had no hope of righting her sleeping pattern in a single day. "Especially if I'm to attend a ball tomorrow evening." She picked up the parcel and started to head from the room.

"Wait right there," Harlen ordered.

She turned to face her grandfather.

"We received word from the Dark Blade Academy yesterday."

She nearly winced at Harlen's tone.

"I spent all yesterday afternoon trying to convince them to let you return. They said you'd been warned enough times." Harlen paused a moment. "Do you have anything to say for yourself?"

Meikah shook her head, trying to suppress her excitement. She doubted that would impress Harlen.

"You should be happy to know that all is not lost. I managed to secure you a place at the Spellsword Academy," Harlen said. "Breena mentioned you need to learn how to control your magic. They'll be able to teach you that there."

Meikah stared at him speechlessly. Somehow she eventually managed to make a comment in answer to his expectant expression. "You did?"

"Yes." He turned to Breena. "Sirena and I will return tomorrow evening to make sure Meikah is dressed properly. It takes more than a gown to be ready for a ball. And I'm sure the Duke and Duchess aren't expecting her to turn up unchaperoned. We'll take her in our carriage." Harlen strode from the room before anyone could argue.

For a few seconds, Meikah was horrified at the thought of her grandparents accompanying her, then laughter bubbled up. What would they say if Kellan had a prank planned for the evening? Shaking her head in answer to her parents' questions, Meikah strolled from the room, smiling. It was sure to be an interesting evening. The smile momentarily dimmed as she thought of the Spellsword Academy. It didn't take long for the smile to return. She'd managed to be thrown out of one academy. How hard could it be to get thrown out of a second one? Still smiling, she headed up the stairs to her room. She needed a sleep. There was still so much to be done.

Free Ebook

Subscribe to Avril's newsletter and receive a free ebook. This ebook is exclusive to those on her mailing list. To find out more about this offer visit:

www.avrilsabine.com/free-ebook

*

We value your privacy and will not sell, rent, exchange or loan your email address to third parties. Your information is confidential and you are under no obligation to remain on the mailing list and can unsubscribe at any time.

Acknowledgements

As always, many thanks to my usual crew. Without you, this book would contain typos, errors and plot holes. Your help is invaluable.

To The Reader

If you enjoyed this book, why not consider leaving a review to help other readers discover it too? Reader engagement is one of the few ways that lets an author know readers want more books in a particular series or genre. So leave a review and tell friends, not only about this book but also about other ones you've enjoyed, so you can continue to enjoy books by your favourite authors for years to come.

Dreams are meant to be lived,

Avril.

The Author

Avril is an Australian author who lives with her family on acreage in South East Queensland. She writes mostly young adult and children's speculative fiction, but has been known to dabble in other genres. You can find more information about her at www.avrilsabine.com where you can also subscribe to her newsletter to be kept informed about new releases, current projects, blog posts and exclusive news.

Titles By Avril Sabine

Stories about strong characters and characters who discover their strengths.

SERIES

Assassins Of The Dead- Young Adult Fantasy/ Paranormal

Book 1: Dark Blade

Book 2: Dragon Touched

Book 3: Society Against Vampires

Book 4: King's Request

Dragon Blood- Young Adult Urban Fantasy (with elements of romance)

(5 book series)

Book 1: Pliethin

Book 2: Wyvern

Book 3: Surety

Book 4: Knight

Book 5: Mage

Dragon Mage- Young Adult Urban Fantasy (with elements of romance)

(Series two of Dragon Blood series)

Book 1: Promise

Dragon Blood Chronicles- Young Adult Urban Fantasy (with elements of romance)

(Companion stand alone series to Dragon Blood)

Book 1: Oath

Book 2: Betrayed

Guardians Of The Round Table- Young Adult Fantasy LitRPG

(Co-written with Storm and Rhys Petersen)

Book 1: Dexterity Fail

Book 2: Goblin Boots

Book 3: Singed Feathers

Book 4: Frog Mage

Book 5: Crystal Mine

Book 6: Cursed Harp

Rosie's Rangers- Young Adult Western Steampunk

(6 book series)

Book 1: Justice

Book 2: Vengeance

Book 3: Treachery

Book 4: Accused

Book 5: Wanted

Book 6: Corruption

Mark Of Kings- Children's Fantasy

(Upper middle grade/preteen)

(4 book series)

Book 1: The Arena

Book 2: The Island

Book 3: The Assassin

Book 4: The King

STAND ALONE SERIES

***Demon Hunters- Young Adult Urban Fantasy/
Horror (with elements of romance)***

Book 1: Blood Sacrifice

Book 2: Retribution

Book 3: Tainted

Book 4: Premonition

Book 5: Cursed

Book 6: Feud

Book 7: Extrication

Plea Of The Damned- Young Adult Urban Fantasy/Paranormal

(6 book series)

Book 1: Forgive Me Lucy

Book 2: Forgive Me Aiden

Book 3: Forgive Me Jena

Book 4: Forgive Me Kobe

Book 5: Forgive Me Marti

Book 6: Forgive Me Dawson

Realms Of The Fae- Young Adult Urban Fantasy (with elements of romance)

The Sword (short story in Like A Girl Anthology)

Heart Of Stone

Book 1: A Debt Owed

Book 2: Marked By The Hunt

Book 3: The Magic Collector

Book 4: An Unexpected Betrayal

Book 5: Imprisoned By Iron

Fairytales Retold (Short Stories)

Snow-White And Rose-Red

The Twelve Brothers

The Light Princess

Beauty And The Beast

Sleeping Beauty

Aschenputtel

The Golden Bird

The Frog Prince

The Death Of Koshchei The Deathless

Myths And Legends Retold (Short Stories)

Ion, Son Of Apollo

Sir Gawain And The Maid With The Narrow Sleeves

Princess Ilse, The Giant's Daughter

YOUNG ADULT NOVELS

Young Adult Fantasy (with elements of romance)

Elf Sight

Earth Bound

Young Adult Urban Fantasy

Stone Warrior (with elements of romance)

The Jungle Inside

Young Adult Contemporary (with elements of romance)

Through Your Eyes

The Ugly Stepsister

Perfect Little Princess

Young Adult Contemporary/Paranormal

Whispers In The Dark (with elements of romance and same sex relationships)

Over Too Soon (with elements of romance)

Young Adult Sci-Fi

Experiment X-One-Six (Urban Sci-Fi/Superheroes)

An Endless Dawn (Post Apocalyptic Sci-Fi)

CHILDREN'S BOOKS

Dragon Lord (Preteen/early teens) (Fantasy)

The Irish Wizard (Upper middle grade) (Urban Fantasy)

SHORT STORIES

Urban Fantasy

Eternally Late

Dealings With Joe

Glimpses (short story in That Moment When Anthology)

Contemporary

The Brat Next Door

Fantasy LitRPG

(Set in the same world as Guardians Of The Round Table Series)

Tales Of Inadon 1: The Disc (Co-written with Storm and Rhys Petersen) (short story in Game On! Anthology)

Post Apocalyptic Sci-Fi

Compulsive Directive

NONFICTION

A Year Of Weekly Writing Exercises (Creative Writing)

Cooking For Families With Allergies (Cooking) (Co-written with Storm Petersen)

Tell Me A Story, Grandma (Memoir)

For the most up to date details on available titles visit:

www.avrilsabine.com/books/bibliography

Assassins Of The Dead Series

To learn more about this series visit:

www.avrilsabine.com/series/aotd

BOOKS AVAILABLE IN THE ASSASSINS OF THE DEAD SERIES

Book 1: Dark Blade

Book 2: Dragon Touched

Book 3: Society Against Vampires

Book 4: King's Request

Disclaimer

This is a work of fiction. Names, characters, businesses, places, events and incidents are either the products of the author's imagination or used in a fictitious manner. Any resemblance to actual persons, living or dead, or actual events is purely coincidental. The opinions expressed or beliefs held are those of the characters and should not be assumed to be the opinions or beliefs of the author.